Nancy Drew®
in
The Secret of Mirror Bay

D1337703

This Armada book belongs to:

_____

_____

_____

Nancy Drew Mystery Stories® in Armada

1 The Secret of Shadow Ranch
2 The Mystery of the 99 Steps
3 Mystery at the Ski Jump
4 The Spider Sapphire Mystery
5 The Clue in the Crossword Cipher
6 The Quest of the Missing Map
7 The Clue in the Old Stagecoach
8 The Clue of the Broken Locket
9 The Message in the Hollow Oak
10 The Invisible Intruder
11 The Ghost of Blackwood Hall
12 Password to Larkspur Lane
13 The Bungalow Mystery
14 The Whispering Statue
15 The Haunted Showboat
16 The Clue of the Dancing Puppet
17 The Clue of the Tapping Heels
18 The Clue in the Crumbling Wall
19 The Mystery of the Tolling Bell
20 The Clue of the Black Keys
21 The Clue of the Leaning Chimney
22 The Scarlet Slipper Mystery
23 The Secret of the Golden Pavilion
24 The Secret in the Old Attic
25 The Ringmaster's Secret
26 Nancy's Mysterious Letter
27 The Phantom of Pine Hill
28 The Mystery of the Fire Dragon
29 The Mystery of the Moss-Covered Mansion
30 The Hidden Staircase

31 The Mystery of the Ivory Charm
32 The Mystery of the Brass-Bound Trunk
33 The Clue of the Velvet Mask
34 The Clue in the Old Album
35 The Witch Tree Symbol
36 The Moonstone Castle Mystery
37 The Secret of Mirror Bay
38 The Double Jinx Mystery
39 Mystery of the Glowing Eye
40 The Secret of the Forgotten City
*
51 The Triple Hoax
52 The Flying Saucer Mystery
53 The Secret in the Old Lace
54 The Greek Symbol Mystery
55 The Swami's Ring
56 The Kachina Doll Mystery
57 The Twin Dilemma
58 The Captive Witness
59 The Mystery of the Winged Lion
60 Race Against Time
61 The Sinister Omen
62 The Elusive Heiress
63 The Clue in the Ancient Disguise
64 The Broken Anchor
65 The Silver Cobweb
66 The Haunted Carousel
67 Enemy Match
68 The Mysterious Image
69 The Emerald-Eyed Cat Mystery
70 The Eskimo's Secret
71 The Bluebeard Room
72 The Phantom of Venice

*For contractual reasons, Armada has been obliged to publish from No. 51 onwards before publishing Nos. 41–50. These missing numbers will be published as soon as possible.

Nancy Drew Mystery Stories®

The Secret of
Mirror Bay

Carolyn Keene

Armada

First published in the U.K. in 1979 by
William Collins Sons & Co. Ltd, London and Glasgow
First published in Armada in 1986
This impression 1987

Armada is an imprint of
the Children's Division, part of
the Collins Publishing Group,
8 Grafton Street, London W1X 3LA

Printed and bound in Great Britain by
William Collins Sons & Co. Ltd, Glasgow

Contents

1 Vacation Hoax 9
2 News of a Sorcerer 17
3 Yo 23
4 The Green Apparition 30
5 A Rescue 37
6 The Cardiff Giant 43
7 Scuba Search 50
8 Bess's Fright 57
9 Bat Attack 64
10 Footprint Lesson 73
11 Valentine Clue 81
12 Firefly Secrets 88
13 The Vanishing Spook 95
14 Overboard! 101
15 Burglars! 108
16 A Valuable Witness 115
17 The Girl Captive 122
18 A Cage of Light 129
19 Trapped! 136
20 A Royal Finish 142

*Nancy dived down and desperately tried to free the
drowning woman!*

·1·

Vacation Hoax

"IT's beautiful!"

"What is?"

"It's spooky!"

"What's spooky?"

"It's fun but it's dangerous!" Nancy Drew smiled at her two friends Bess and George who were listening intently.

George Fayne spoke up. She was a tall, slender athletic girl who loved her boyish name.

"You forgot to say it's intriguing, but what is and where is it?"

"The spot we're going to," Nancy replied. "That is, you girls are invited to join me. I hope you can come."

Nancy went on to say that Aunt Eloise Drew, her father's sister who lived in New York City, had rented a cottage on a bay. "The name of the cabin is Mirror Bay Bide-A-Wee."

Bess Marvin, blonde, pretty, and always talking about going on a diet, looked at Nancy puzzled. "The place sounds wonderful. What did you mean by all those things you were saying about it?"

Nancy, slim and attractive-looking with reddish

blonde hair, said, "There's a mystery, of course. Aunt Eloise heard that early on misty mornings a woman is seen gliding over the water."

"In what?" George queried.

"Oh, she's walking," Nancy replied.

"How could she?" George asked sceptically.

"That's one thing I want to find out," Nancy answered. "The lake, of which the bay is a part, is a hundred and sixty-seven feet deep in the middle."

"Wow!" Bess exclaimed. "Dangerous spot to fall overboard with heavy shoes on."

Nancy said the water was shallow near shore and gradually became deeper. Bess and George, who were cousins, asked where the lake was.

"In New York State," Nancy told them. "The Indians called the lake Otesaga and there's a lovely hotel named after it. Later James Fenimore Cooper wrote stories about settlers and Indians in the area. He found the water so much like a mirror that he called it Glimmerglass. Now the official name for it is Otsego Lake."

Nancy explained that at the southern end of the lake was the famous village of Cooperstown.

George's eyes lit up. "That's where the Baseball Hall of Fame is."

"Right," Nancy replied, "and there are also many interesting museums in and around Cooperstown."

"Sounds great to me," Bess remarked. "When would we go?"

"Tomorrow morning," Nancy replied. "Aunt Eloise is taking a bus to Cooperstown from New York. We're to meet her there and drive along the water to Hyde Bay, then walk down to Bide-A-Wee cabin."

"Bide-A-Wee," said Bess. "That's Scottish for 'stay awhile', isn't it?"

"Yes," Nancy agreed. "Well, how about you girls getting on the phone and finding out if you can go with me?"

It took less than ten minutes for the cousins to call their parents and get permission. They hurried home to pack and Nancy went out to the kitchen to talk to the Drew's housekeeper, Hannah Gruen.

Mrs Gruen had been with the family since the death of Mrs Drew when Nancy was only three years old. The tender-hearted woman was like a mother to her and was very proud of Nancy's accomplishments as a young amateur detective. Nevertheless, she was always a little fearful when Nancy set off on one of her sleuthing expeditions.

"Do you know what I heard?" she asked. "That there are bears in the woods of the Cooperstown area. You'd better be careful if you go up in the mountains."

Nancy laughed. "Suppose I carry a few combs of honey with me," she teased. "If a bear comes my way, I'll toss one at him."

Hannah Gruen smiled. "You always know what to do," she said.

Nancy's father was out of town, but the next morning she said goodbye to him on the telephone. Tall, handsome Carson Drew was a well-known lawyer in River Heights. She picked up Bess and George in her convertible and they set off for Cooperstown.

The long drive in the fresh summer air was delightful. They stopped for lunch at a wayside snack bar. Soon after starting off again, they were confronted with a long detour.

"Oh dear!" said Nancy. "We'll have to go miles out of our way and be late meeting Aunt Eloise. I just hate to think of her waiting on the sidewalk with her luggage."

"Maybe she'll go to the lovely hotel you mentioned," Bess suggested.

Nancy shook her head. "Not if I know Aunt Eloise. She'll be right at the bus stop."

Nancy put on all the speed the law allowed and finally pulled into the main street of Cooperstown twenty minutes late.

"My goodness, what's going on?" Bess asked.

Along one kerb stood five large buses. People were milling about the street, arguing and making threats to no one in particular. There were suitcases and bags strewn on the pavement. Shop-keepers had come outside to learn what the trouble was.

Nancy parked some distance from the commotion, locked the car, and the three girls hurried up the street. They saw Aunt Eloise standing in the doorway of a shop guarding her own luggage.

"Nancy!" exclaimed the tall charming woman, who taught school in New York.

The three girls kissed her, then asked what was going on.

"Right after my regularly scheduled bus arrived here," she said, "this group of charter buses drove in. These people were aboard. As I understand the story, they had been sold tickets in New York City for a week's stay at a very elegant place called The Homestead on the Mountain. The round trip and all hotel expenses were only a hundred dollars per person. But now it seems the hotel reservation was a hoax. There is no such place here as The Homestead on the Mountain."

"How dreadful!" said Bess. "Who's responsible for this?"

Miss Drew said she did not know. The bus drivers claimed to be entirely innocent. Their company had been paid for making the charter trip from New York City. The agitated passengers looked closely at their brochures of the trip and now they discovered that the tickets did not include a return trip, even though they had been promised one.

"It's an outrage!" screamed a red-faced woman.

Just then one of the irate men spotted Nancy. In a couple of leaps he was at her side and grabbing her shoulder.

"Here she is!" he shouted. "The faker!"

Nancy removed the man's hand and stared at him. "What are you talking about?" she asked.

By this time a crowd of people was running towards the girl. Someone exclaimed, "She's the one all right!"

Aunt Eloise stepped forward. "I demand to know what you're accusing my niece of."

The man pulled a travel brochure from his pocket. He pointed to a reproduction of a photograph. The pamphlet was printed on the kind of paper used for newspapers and the picture was not distinct. It showed a round-faced man and a girl who certainly did resemble Nancy.

"There's your proof!" the irate passenger said to Aunt Eloise. "Get the police, somebody!"

There was no need to summon them. Two State Police officers were already on hand and pushing their way through the crowd.

"What's going on here?" one of them demanded.

The man from New York answered. "This girl sold me a phony ticket and I want my money back."

Aunt Eloise, Bess, and George exclaimed in unison, "She did not! There is some mistake!"

One of the officers faced Nancy. "What do you have to say?"

Quickly Nancy explained that evidently some girl who resembled her, and a man partner, had cheated all these people out of a vacation. She ended by saying, "I had nothing to do with it. My friends and I just arrived in a car. This is my aunt. She has rented a cottage on the bay and we're about to go there."

The adamant passenger pushed the brochure and his hotel reservation towards the policeman.

"Don't pay any attention to what they say. Here's proof!"

The two officers stared at the photograph, then one said he thought that while the girl did resemble Nancy she was no doubt someone else. He asked to see Nancy's driver's licence. Bess, George, and Aunt Eloise also showed theirs.

The angry man moved away. He seemed unconvinced and cried out, "What's to become of us? We paid all this money and we have no place to stay and no ride back to New York."

The officer said he would see what he could do to help the stranded travellers. He smiled at Aunt Eloise. "I'm sorry you people had such an unfortunate welcome to Cooperstown. I hope your stay here will be so enjoyable you will forget what happened."

Miss Drew thanked him and turned away from the crowd. The girls picked up her luggage and headed for the car.

Aunt Eloise pointed across the street. A man was just entering a restaurant.

"That's my bus driver," she said.

"Um! Handsome," Bess murmured.

The others smiled. Miss Drew directed her niece to East Lake Road, which ran a few hundred feet above the lake.

On their left was the mirror-like water. Here and there a sailboat went by, wafted by a lazy breeze. Along the shore were several camps where children were swimming. Sounds of laughter came up the hillside.

To the right of the road was a steep wooded hillside, broken only now and then by a house or a garage. Some six miles from town they came to a small parking area on their left and climbed out of the car. They gathered their bags and trudged down the path leading to the waterfront. Soon an attractive cabin came into view. Though on the bay it was near the point where the inlet joined the lake proper.

"Welcome to Mirror Bay Bide-A-Wee," said Aunt Eloise. "I hope you girls will have a glorious time and solve the mystery of the woman who can glide over the water."

The cabin was rustic and had a large front porch with a view west across the lake and north across the bay. Besides a living room with a huge fireplace and a well-furnished kitchen, there were three good-sized bedrooms. Miss Drew assigned Nancy to one, the cousins to another, and the third to herself. As soon as the hot weary travellers had unpacked, they put on bathing suits and went for a swim.

"What gorgeous water!" George exclaimed, doing a fast crawl towards the middle of the sparkling lake.

"Come back!" cried Bess. "There's enough water around here to swim in!"

George turned back. "Bet I could swim all the way to the west bank of the lake without stopping," she said. "Oh, how I hate myself!" She grinned.

Refreshed and hungry, the girls insisted that Aunt Eloise sit on the porch and enjoy the brilliant sunset while they prepared supper.

"I wonder," Nancy added, "where that girl is who resembles me. I hope she doesn't show up around this area."

"Oh, she wouldn't dare!" Bess warned.

The group went to bed early and slept soundly. Nancy awoke early, raised up from her bed, and looked out of the window towards the water. It was very misty.

"Maybe that woman who glides over the water is out there now," she thought. "Anyway, it won't hurt to look. It's possible the story was made up just to amuse tourists."

Quietly Nancy arose, put on her slippers, and walked to the porch. Suddenly she gave a start. Was her imagination playing tricks, or did she really see a ghostly figure gliding over the water?

·2·

News of a Sorcerer

THOUGH Nancy left the cabin quickly and hurried down the steps to the waterfront, she could see no one in the mist. Had the woman gone out too far from shore to be noticed?

Perplexed, the young detective kept on staring ahead. Very slowly the mist was beginning to rise. She could gaze through it more plainly now. She looked in every direction. The woman was not in sight at the moment.

"If I really saw someone, where could she have gone?" Nancy asked herself.

Then another thought came to Nancy. The ghostly figure may have seen her coming and swum away under water.

As her eyes searched the surface, the young detective spotted a piece of paper floating near shore. Wondering what it was, and if by any chance the spectral figure could have dropped it, Nancy waded into the water to retrieve it. The paper proved to be part of a letter.

Nancy carried it to the porch and dried the torn sheet the best she could with a tissue. Most of the letter was illegible but part of one sentence stood out clearly. It read:

With tears the poor child's coach was
lowered near—

"Strange!" Nancy thought. "What does it mean?"

As she sat on a rocker cogitating, Aunt Eloise came outside. "Oh, here you are!" she said. "I noticed your bed was empty and wondered where you'd gone."

Nancy kissed her aunt good morning, then told of her adventure. "Make a guess as to what those strange words mean," she teased.

Miss Drew laughed. "I wouldn't have the faintest idea. But you'll solve the mystery. You always do."

She bent down and put an arm affectionately around her niece. Nancy hoped that what her aunt had just said would come true.

Solving mysteries was not new to Nancy. From the time her father had suggested she assist him in uncovering *The Secret of Shadow Ranch,* right through to the intriguing case of *The Moonstone Castle Mystery*, she had met with success.

"Will I be so lucky this time?" Nancy asked herself.

A few minutes later Bess and George came out to the porch and were shown the strange paper.

"Sounds gruesome," Bess remarked. "Did that phantom woman on the water drop it?"

Nancy told the girls what little she knew. "In any case I'd like to find the owner of this paper and perhaps learn what it means."

"How can you?" Bess asked. "You haven't a single clue except a misty woman."

Nancy smiled but did not reply. Aunt Eloise suggested that they all dress and get breakfast. "Maybe by that time an answer will come to Nancy. By the way,

I'm going into town for food supplies. You girls won't need the car, will you?"

"No," Nancy answered. "What I'd like to do is go all around the neighbourhood and question everybody about this paper. The owner may be nearby."

After Aunt Eloise had left, the three girls tidied the cabin, locked it, and trudged up the hill to the road. They turned right towards Cooperstown and presently met a group of boy campers on a hike with an instructor.

Nancy asked the affable young man if he knew anyone who had lost part of a letter.

"No, I don't," he answered. "Did you find one?"

"Yes." Nancy inquired if the instructor had heard the story of the woman who glided on the water.

He and the little boys began to laugh. "Yes, we've all heard it," he said. "Of course no one believes the story but it's a good one."

He changed the subject abruptly, asking where the girls were staying. When Nancy told him, the young man remarked, "Don't be surprised if some of us come to call on you. Mirror Bay Bide-A-Wee is known as a refreshment stop."

Bess dimpled. "Oh, is that why there's a refrigerator full of soft drinks in the corner of the porch?"

The instructor and the boys nodded.

George grinned. "If you do stop by, be sure to bring a clue with you about the misty woman."

The young man laughed and walked off with the boys.

Presently the girls reached a settlement of cabins which sprawled down the hillside from the road to the water. The threesome stopped at each cabin and inquired if anyone there had lost part of a torn letter.

No one had, and most of the summer residents seemed amused by the idea.

"Let's go back," Bess begged. "We aren't learning a thing."

Nancy agreed, although she hated to give up the search. When they reached the cabin, George said she was going swimming.

"I want to try gliding over the water," she said.

"I dare you!" Nancy said as they went into their rooms.

The three girls changed hurriedly, ran down to the water, and swam around a little while. Then Nancy stopped to examine the shoreline. She detected footprints but they did not seem to go anywhere.

Just then George called out, "Nancy, look! I'm gliding on the water!"

Nancy turned. Sure enough, her friend was actually skimming on the top of the bay! Before Nancy had a chance to figure this out, George suddenly dived in and Bess's head and shoulders appeared.

Nancy burst into laughter. "Good trick!" she called. "You had me fooled for a moment. Nice work, Bess. You did well holding your breath that long and carrying George across the water on your shoulders."

"I couldn't have held out another second," Bess told her. "Next time we try that stunt, I'll do the gliding and George can be under water."

Her cousin groaned. "I may be strong, but I'd have to be Supergirl to hold your weight!" she remarked.

Bess quickly dunked George before she could swim away. Nancy laughed, then sobered. She suddenly had an idea. Could this be the way the phantom woman accomplished her unusual walk?

She mentioned this to the girls and added, "But what is the purpose of it?"

Bess gave a great sigh. "We haven't been here twenty-four hours. I just feel the holiday spirit too much to figure out such a problem. Besides, I'm starving. Let's start lunch."

The girls had just finished preparing a delicious fruit-and-cottage cheese salad when Aunt Eloise appeared. She was laden down with bags of food.

"Goodness!" George cried. "There's enough here for an army!"

Bess's eyes were glistening. "Um!" she said, taking out jars of jam and jelly. "Peach preserves and pineapple—"

George gave her cousin a stern look. "You sound like someone in an eating contest. Take it easy."

Aunt Eloise put a stop to the needling by saying she had two surprises to tell the girls. "First of all, I've rented a sailboat for you to use while you're here."

"How wonderful!" Nancy exclaimed. "Oh, you're such a darling!" She gave her aunt a great hug.

Miss Drew went on to say that the sailboat, the *Crestwood*, was at the main Cooperstown dock.

"Let's go down this afternoon and get it," George said enthusiastically. "It sounds great!"

"Aunt Eloise," Nancy said, "while we're eating, tell us about the second surprise."

Miss Drew nodded. "This one is not in the line of fun. I'm afraid it could mean danger to you."

"How?"

Her aunt said that just as she was leaving town, she had seen a girl hurrying along the shore road. "Later I realized she resembles you very much. I wonder if she could be the one who was part of that vacation swindle."

Nancy frowned. Her aunt could be right. The police were looking for the girl. It could mean more problems for Nancy if she were mistaken again for this lawbreaker.

"I'll certainly have to watch out," she said aloud.

At two o'clock Aunt Eloise and the girls started for town in the car. Part way there, where the wooded mountain rose steeply from the road, the air suddenly reverberated with an anguished cry for help.

Nancy stopped the car and asked, "Where did that come from?"

The cry was repeated but the listeners could not be sure whether it was coming from the mountain or from the area between the road and the shoreline. Nancy pulled to the side of the road and parked. Everyone got out.

"Let's split up for the search," Nancy suggested. "Aunt Eloise, suppose you and Bess go down towards the shore. George and I will climb the mountain."

The two search parties started off at once. Nancy and George had not gone very far into the woods when they saw a girl racing pell-mell down the hill. She was about twenty years old and very pretty. But now she looked terrified and kept glancing back over her shoulder.

"What's the matter?" Nancy called to her.

The girl was nearly breathless when she reached Nancy and George but she managed to gasp out, "The sorcerer! It's true! He's up there! Don't go any farther!"

·3·

Yo

"YOU'RE safe now!" Nancy assured the distraught girl. The young detective put an arm around the stranger's waist and George held her hand.

"Yes, you're perfectly safe now," George reiterated. "We have a car down below. Would you like to sit in it and rest awhile?"

The girl heaved a great sigh. "That won't be necessary. I must return to camp." She pointed in the distance towards the water. "I'm an instructor down there. Perhaps I shouldn't have gone wandering so far by myself."

"We'll drive you back," Nancy offered. "A few minutes ago you were warning us not to go up the mountain. Why?"

"Because there's a real sorcerer up there—a horrible-looking creature. I suppose he's a man—but awfully scary in appearance. He wears a green costume that makes him blend into the foliage. There's a funny green light glowing about him. That's not so bad, but his face—it has a weird greenish hue."

"What about his hair?" Nancy asked. She was intrigued by the description of this creature.

"I don't remember seeing any. I guess his costume

had a hood." The girl sighed. "To tell the truth, I was so frightened I nearly froze in my tracks.

"He didn't come any closer but pointed a finger down the mountainside and said, 'Go! Do not return or I will change your bones into stone so you will never walk again!' "

The girl had been trembling with fear, but suddenly she shook off the mood.

"What a ninny I am!" she chided herself. "Of course there are no such things as sorcerers. Don't ever tell my little girl campers that I thought one frightened me! By the way, my name is Karen Jones. What are yours?"

Nancy and George introduced themselves and said they were glad Karen was over her scare. Nevertheless, they were sure that she had seen some man with a greenish face and wearing a green suit. No doubt he had turned a flashlight on himself.

"Did you see anything else on the mountain?" Nancy asked Karen.

"Nothing special. You mean like a hut or a tent? No, I didn't see anything like that. But tell me, why do you suppose that man is pulling such a stunt?"

George smiled. "I'd say to keep people away from himself and whatever he's doing in the forest." The three girls started walking towards the car.

Karen's eyes grew large. "Do you think something illegal is going on up in the mountain?"

"Could be," George replied.

Karen sighed again. "At college I'm a botany student. I was up in the forest hunting for luminescent mushrooms on tree stumps. You know, the kind that glow."

"I've heard of them," Nancy told her, "but I've never seen any."

"This coming term I'm specializing in fungi," Karen explained, "and I'm supposed to hunt for something luminescent this summer. But I wouldn't go up that mountain again for a million dollars!"

"I don't blame you," George said "But if you do, better take a crowd with you and not your campers either."

By this time the three had reached the car. Bess and Aunt Eloise were just returning from the waterfront and reported that the cry for help had not come from there.

"It was on the mountain," Nancy explained, then introduced Karen to the others.

George gave a quick résumé of the instructor's story.

"Oh, how horrible!" Bess exclaimed.

They all got into the car and headed for Karen's camp.

On the way she said, "One day I met a boy—he's really a young man—in Cooperstown who told me there was a sorcerer on the mountain. He works at the main boat dock and people around there laugh at him and say he's full of tall tales and that this was just another one of them. But now I believe him."

Nancy asked who the boy was.

"His name is Johann Bradley, but everybody calls him Yo," Karen explained. "I got the impression that he's older than he looks and is a town character."

By this time they had reached Karen's camp and she got out of the car. "I can't thank you girls enough. If you ever learn the mystery of the green man, let me know."

"I will," Nancy replied as she locked the door and drove off.

During the rest of the ride to town, the conversation centred around the strange person in the woods. Who was he? Why was he there? Was he a danger to the community?

Bess spoke up. "I thought Mirror Bay Bide-A-Wee was going to be as calm as the water here and in less than two days we've bumped into two mysteries."

Aunt Eloise laughed. "Which I'm sure pleases Nancy very much."

Nancy grinned. "I'll be happier after I solve them. I'm going to start by interviewing the boy, Yo."

She drove immediately to the Cooperstown main boat dock. Before taking the sailboat, she asked the man at the booth if Yo were around. He pointed to the end of a dock where a round-faced, pudgy young man sat twirling a toothpick in his fingers. As Nancy came closer, she could hear low singing. His voice was melodious and dreamy.

When Nancy approached, Yo looked up but did not arise.

"Are you Yo?" she asked.

"That's me," the young man replied. "Something I can do for you?"

Nancy sat down beside him.

"Yo," she began, "a girl at a camp along the lake told me you've seen a man with a strange green face and wearing a green suit up on the mountain. He had a light around him."

"That's right. But he didn't scare me," Yo bragged, grinning.

"Do you know who the man is or anything about him?"

"Nothing except he's a sorcerer," Yo answered. "As

you get near him he'll tell you awful things. Like what he said to me. 'Jump in the lake, boy, and don't come up!' "

"Nice person," Nancy commented. "Can you tell me anything else about him? Does he live on the mountain?"

"Search me. I know these mountains pretty well and I've never seen a shack around that area where he rushed at me. Maybe he comes from a distance."

"But why would he always appear in that particular spot?" Nancy asked.

"I don't know." Abruptly Yo changed the subject. "You and your friends are newcomers here, aren't you? I saw you at the bus stop yesterday. Did you get taken, too, by those phony people?"

"No," Nancy told him. "That was a crime! By the way, the girl involved is supposed to resemble me. Have you seen her around?"

"Yup. Lots of times."

Nancy was surprised to hear this. "Do you mean she lives here?"

Yo said he did not know, but he had often seen her walk up East Lake Road and take off through the forest.

Nancy wondered if there might be some connection between her and the green man. Was he the girl's partner in the vacation racket? Perhaps a gang of them was hiding on the mountain! She said nothing of this to Yo and after a few minutes more conversation she finally stood up.

"What's your name?" Yo asked. "And where are you staying?"

Nancy told him, thinking if she did not, he would find out anyway through the rental record of the sailboat.

She also mentioned her aunt and the other girls who were with her.

"Yo, the police are looking for that girl who resembles me. If you see her around again, you had better tell them."

"Okay, I will," he promised. "Now you got me interested. I wonder who she is."

Yo got up and accompanied Nancy back to the booth where Aunt Eloise was making arrangements about the sailboat.

Hearing this, Yo asked Nancy, "Do you know how to sail?"

"Oh yes," she replied.

. The pudgy young man smiled to himself. Nancy wondered what he was thinking about, but he gave no explanation.

Instead, he said, "I got a great little boat with an outboard motor. I'll stop by your place sometime and show it to you."

He was introduced to Miss Drew, Bess, and George. Then, smiling, Yo walked off.

"So he's the tall-story boy," George remarked.

Bess said, "Perhaps they're not tall stories. Maybe they're true. I don't think Karen was making up what she told us." Bess gave a great sigh and said in a dramatic voice, "That old mountain is spooky!"

The others laughed, then discussed who would take the sailboat up to Mirror Bay Bide-A-Wee. It was finally decided that Nancy and George would. Bess and Aunt Eloise would return by car.

As the two girls set off, Nancy kept thinking about the funny smile on Yo's face. Did the lake and the bay have tricky winds? Would she and George be likely to run into some kind of trouble? Or did Yo know something more about the mountain he was not telling?

·4·

The Green Apparition

As the sailboat moved up the lake, Nancy relaxed. It was a beautiful day and the water was calm. There was just enough breeze to carry the craft along at moderate speed. The girls had a close look at Kingfisher Tower and Council Rock, famous in the Indian history of Otsego.

"At the head of this nine-mile-long lake," said Nancy, pointing ahead, "is Mount Wellington but it's never called that. Instead, the mountain is known as Sleeping Lion because of its shape."

"And it certainly looks like one," George observed.

Nancy explained, "I've been reading up on the history of this place. Did you know that the village was founded by William Cooper, father of James Fenimore Cooper? He later became a judge. There's an amusing story told in connection with his wife. He loved the wilderness and when he was a young man he decided to move his family from Burlington, New Jersey, up to Cooperstown.

"She refused and would not budge from her favourite chair. Not to be outwitted, Cooper had his wife and the chair lifted bodily into a covered wagon and brought to her new home."

George laughed heartily. "I'll bet she loved that! If my husband ever dared do that to me, I wouldn't speak to him for a month!"

"I'll remind your friend Burt," Nancy teased.

George grimaced, then said, "Here's a local story I heard. There was a man named Prevost who lived along the east shore of this lake. He wrote to a friend, saying all his children had 'whooping cough' at the same time. Ordinarily this might not seem like anything unusual, but as it happened, Mr Prevost had twentyone children!"

It was Nancy's turn to laugh. By this time the girls were nearing the bay. Suddenly both of them noticed two boys in a canoe.

They were clawing furiously at the water to reach the paddles which evidently had been swept from their craft. Their efforts seemed futile, so Nancy suggested to George that they help the little fellows.

"I'll come about," she said, "and slacken the sheet rope."

George worked the tiller. By expert tacking, the girls came alongside the drifting paddles and scooped them up. The boys were waiting with outstretched hands.

"That's great!" one of the little fellows exclaimed. "Gee, thanks a lot."

George grinned. "You boys are really good at dog-paddling," she remarked.

"Yeah, but pretty soon your arms ache," the other boy said.

Nancy asked them if they ever went up into the woods on the mountain.

"Sure," said one lad, who told them his name was Chuck.

"Have you ever seen a strange man up there?" Nancy queried.

"No," Chuck answered, "but we've heard funny sounds."

Nancy asked what they were like.

"Something like the whirring of machinery—you know, soft buzzing."

"You have no idea what it was from?"

The boys looked at each other. "Maybe we shouldn't tell you, but we got scared and ran away," Chuck confessed.

Nancy smiled, saying she did not blame them. Then she asked, "Have you ever seen a woman gliding across the water near here?"

Both boys giggled, and Chuck said, "You must be kidding!"

The children thanked the girls again for retrieving the paddles and started off. Nancy and George pulled into the dock of Mirror Bay Bide-A-Wee a few minutes later. Aunt Eloise and Bess were waiting for them.

"The *Crestwood* is great!" Nancy told her aunt. "What a wonderful surprise for us!" Then she spoke of Yo's strange smile and tried to guess why.

Aunt Eloise said that Yo seemed a little hard to figure out. "If you'd given him the chance, he might have told you some tall story about the *Crestwood*."

Bess announced that she was hot from her trip to the village and wanted to go for a swim. "How about the rest of you?" she asked.

Everyone was willing and within minutes they were ready. Nancy proposed that they do a little diving to see if they could find out what the woman gliding on the water might have been looking for.

"I'm sure she was searching for something because she kept her head down and turned it from side to side."

The girls separated and went underwater time after time. The bay was so clear they could see as deep as the sun filtered. They tried scratching the silt and loose shale, but found nothing of interest.

In a little while, however, George came to the surface. "I've discovered something!" she exclaimed, and led the way down to a sunken rowing-boat.

It took the combined efforts of them all during the short periods when they could hold their breath to turn the rowing-boat over and finally bring it to the surface.

"It still floats!" George remarked. "Do you suppose this is what the woman was looking for?"

Nancy shrugged as they beached the rowing-boat. "In any case, let's examine it."

Both lockers were opened but contained only an assortment of old rags. Nothing was wedged under the slatted floorboards.

"If there was ever anything hidden in this old wreck," said George, "it has long since floated away or been taken."

Nancy agreed. "Let's leave it on the shore so the woman can have a chance to look at it."

Bess spoke up. "You keep referring to that mysterious figure as if she were a real person. I think it's just some funny way the mist rolls in here that makes it look like a woman."

Nancy said nothing but she was convinced a live person was involved.

The group was very hungry and all helped prepare the evening meal. An hour later they began to eat.

"This baked chicken is scrumptious," George complimented Nancy. "You're some cook."

"But it won't match Bess's dessert!" she replied, winking at her friend.

Broad smiles crossed their faces when Bess later came from the kitchen and set down the delectable dish. Atop the thickly frosted chocolate roll were huge walnuts. The first slice was passed to Aunt Eloise.

After tasting it, she announced with a smile, "It's good, but I prefer my walnuts dipped in chocolate rather than pickled."

"Pickled walnuts?" Bess asked incredulously.

Miss Drew nodded. "You got these from a jar I bought in the village. The pickling is based on a colonial recipe. Back in those days preserves and pickles were often made from such foods as green walnuts, barberries, parsley, even nasturtium buds."

After the first bite the diners got used to the unusual taste. As Bess was directing her attention to a second slice of cake, George cast an annoyed glance at her cousin.

"Pretty soon you'll look like a sweet roll!" the slim girl quipped.

"That's not fair, George Fayne," her cousin returned.

Aunt Eloise and Nancy glanced at each other and decided it was time to change the subject.

As the girls finished tidying the kitchen, Nancy said, "Who's game to hike up the mountain and try to prove or disprove the stories of the green sorcerer?"

George was eager to go, but Bess was not keen about it.

"How about you, Aunt Eloise?" Nancy asked. Miss

Drew smiled. "I wouldn't think of letting you go alone, and besides I'm interested in seeing what's up there. Let's all make the climb."

Each carried a flashlight but did not use it at once since it was not yet dusk. The foursome had been climbing for about ten minutes when they heard footsteps. Presently a man came towards them. He was dressed in woodsman's clothes and carried a small bag like those used for tools.

"Good evening," he said pleasantly. Then he added, "Isn't it kind of late for you ladies to be climbing the mountain? There are many holes along this so-called trail. You're lucky you didn't twist an ankle."

Aunt Eloise said, "I'm sure we'll be perfectly all right. We'll be careful."

The man frowned. He was rather short but had an athletic build and looked very strong. "I beg you not to go any farther in the dark. It's too dangerous. I'll be glad to help you down the mountain."

Nancy thanked him for his solicitousness but said they would like to go a little farther. She was tempted to ask him if he had ever seen the green man, yet instinct told her not to.

Without another word the man went on down the mountain trail. Aunt Eloise and the girls climbed upward. Suddenly the woods began to sparkle with infinitesimal lights.

"Fireflies!" Nancy exclaimed. "When we get back, let's gather some in a jar and watch the little insects turn their lights off and on."

The trekkers had gone only a short distance when suddenly they heard a shrill whistle like those used by the police.

"What's that for?" George asked.

"Perhaps it was some kind of a signal," Nancy replied. "The sound seemed to come from below, so maybe the man who passed us blew it to warn some friends who are up here."

Bess looked very unhappy. "I'm sure we're heading for trouble," she insisted. "Please, let's go back to the cabin!"

But she was the only one who wanted to stop the hunt. Contrary to what the man had said, Aunt Eloise and the girls had found no holes. With the glow from their flashlights and the many fireflies, they were able to detect rough spots.

Bess became more and more nervous. "I just know there's danger ahead. Maybe it's only intuition, but I think we should give up!"

Nancy had another idea. "If there are people on the mountain carrying on some illegal operation," she said, "they've certainly been forewarned of the approach of strangers." She suggested that they turn off their flashlights and stop talking. "Let's hide behind trees."

Five minutes later the strange apparition of the green man appeared a little distance ahead. He was swathed in a weird, flickering light, and his face had an eerie, greenish hue.

"Oh!" Bess cried out involuntarily.

At that moment a deep sonorous voice began to speak. Was it coming from the green man or from someone else nearby?

"I am the sorcerer," the voice said. "Return to your cabin at once! Trouble there!"

·5·

A Rescue

BESS was already running pell-mell down the hill, her flashlight pointing the way. "Come on! Hurry!" she cried out.

The other girls seemed mesmerized by the strange figure. Miss Drew insisted that they leave and finally they followed her. Nancy was last in line. She turned to look back.

The green apparition was gone!

Nancy was puzzled. "How did the man accomplish such an instantaneous exit?" she asked herself. "Of course he could have turned out the light surrounding him, but what about his clothing which definitely glowed with a green hue even in the dark?

"I'm coming up here again in the daylight to find out what's going on," she determined.

When the group reached Mirror Bay Bide-A-Wee they were relieved to find the cabin untouched. To be sure there was nothing explosive or otherwise dangerous, they searched every inch of the place, inside and out. They did not come upon anything harmful.

"That sorcerer just wanted to get rid of us," George said in disgust.

"One thing is sure," Nancy remarked. "Yo, Karen,

and all of us have seen the green man, so we know he does exist."

Bess spoke up. "I wish he'd go out of existence and the sooner the better!"

The climb up the mountainside and the quick descent had given everyone an appetite. They enjoyed a late evening snack of cheese and fruit, then went to bed.

Nancy was first to awaken the next morning. It was still early but instantly she thought of the figure that might be gliding across the water.

"Maybe I could see her more clearly this time," she thought and hurried out to the porch.

The mist was not so heavy as the previous day and she could plainly see a woman with greying hair and wearing white slacks and sweater moving across the water.

When Nancy looked more intently, it occurred to her that the figure was not gliding but walking. The stranger kept going out deeper and deeper until the water reached her knees.

"How far is she going?" Nancy wondered.

As the young detective continued to gaze, the woman suddenly lost her balance. She went down under the water. Nancy waited for her to reappear, but there was no sign of her.

"Something has happened!" Nancy decided.

She raced from the porch across the strip of beach and through the shallow water. Still the woman had not reappeared.

"The impact must have knocked her out!" Nancy thought worriedly.

In a frantic lunge she shallow-dived at the point where the woman had gone down. She could see her thrashing with her arms but unable to rise. Nancy rushed towards her and now realised that the woman was wearing knee stilts. One of them had caught between two rocks.

Nancy yanked at the stilt and pulled it loose. To her horror the woman had stopped struggling. She was drowning!

"I must do something quick!" Nancy thought, realizing that soon she would have to go to the surface for air herself.

Nancy attempted to guide the victim to the surface but the load seemed too great. She knew she could not hold out much longer.

At that moment George appeared. She had come to the porch just in time to see Nancy go underwater but fail to reappear quickly. Together the two girls brought the woman to the surface. They towed her to the beach, and Nancy gave her mouth-to-mouth resuscitation.

By this time Bess and Aunt Eloise had come outside and hurried to them. There were anxious moments as the girls took turns giving the victim artificial respiration.

Aunt Eloise had gone for a blanket to cover her. The stilts were unbuckled from just below the woman's knees.

No one had spoken. But when the stranger suddenly took a deep natural breath they all sighed in relief.

"Thank goodness!" said Bess.

The first-aid treatment was continued until the victim was breathing normally again. Her eyelids fluttered open but instantly closed.

Aunt Eloise said, "Let's carry her up to the cot on the porch."

This was done very gently and carefully. They watched the woman intently to see if she would show any signs of going into shock. She did not seem to; instead, she fell into a deep exhausted sleep.

"We can take turns watching her," Nancy said. "In the meantime, let's get dressed and have breakfast."

The woman slept peacefully and Miss Drew thought it was not necessary to call a doctor. Breakfast over, the girls did the necessary housework while Aunt Eloise sat on the porch with the patient.

In the meantime, they had examined the aluminium stilts. They could be adjusted to a six-foot length and had large square ends covered with rubber.

"I guess," said George, "that on land one could walk indefinitely on these. But in the water where there are uneven surfaces, it must be dangerous."

"As the woman found out," Bess remarked. "I take it she doesn't know how to swim and dive, or she wouldn't have needed these. What do you suppose she was hunting for? Surely not that rowing-boat."

"I hope we can find out when she wakes up," Nancy replied.

They went out to the porch and were just in time to see the near-drowning victim open her eyes and keep them open. She looked from one face to another in bewilderment.

Everyone smiled at her and Aunt Eloise said, "You're all right now. You had a nice long nap."

The stranger sat up and it was evident she had regained her strength. She smiled at last and asked, "You rescued me?"

They nodded and introduced themselves.

"Thank you. Thank you very much. That was a

dreadful experience. I shall never go near the water again."

Miss Drew asked, "Would you like some toast and tea?"

"I'm sure that would taste very good. I do feel kind of weak."

While Bess went to prepare the food, their guest told them she was Miss Anne Armitage, a retired school-teacher.

"I'm staying in a little cottage on the west side of the lake. My reason for being here is to find something in this bay."

Miss Armitage did not explain further. Instead, she told the group that as a child she had loved to walk on stilts and became a real expert at it. She had continued to practise.

"Since I can't swim," she said, "I thought I'd use a stilt-method for going into deeper and deeper water. I suppose I was foolish not to use a life jacket."

"I'm afraid you were," Aunt Eloise remarked.

By this time Bess had the toast and tea ready and brought it out to the porch on a tray.

Miss Armitage seemed to enjoy them. As she finished a second cupful, colour came back into her face.

"You are wonderful people," she said. "And very brave too. There is no way I could ever repay your kindness."

"Do you feel like talking and telling us any more about what you're doing?" Aunt Eloise asked.

Miss Armitage smiled. "I suppose it's the least I can do for people who saved my life."

She paused and looked off over the water. Then, as if making up her mind to something, she said, "If all of you will promise to keep a great secret, I will tell you what I'm trying to do. It's a fabulous story."

Each of her listeners agreed to keep the matter confidential and leaned forward expectantly as she began.

·6·

The Cardiff Giant

"ONE of my ancestors," Miss Armitage began, "was an aristocrat in old Czarist Russia. She was very wealthy and owned beautiful things. Much to her family's dismay, she fell in love with an American and came to this country to marry him. They settled in Cooperstown in a large house with attractive grounds. Later the place burned down."

"What a shame!" Bess put in.

"Yes, it was," Miss Armitage agreed. "But long before the fire, the woman had one child—a beautiful little girl. She brought her daughter up as if she were a princess and even imported a child's royal coach from Russia. Her own little pony pulled it."

As Miss Armitage paused, Nancy smiled. "This sounds like some of the fairy tales I used to read."

The visitor nodded. "Indeed it does, and the whole tale fascinates me."

"What's the rest of the story?" George asked. "You haven't told us yet about the bay. Where does that come in?"

Miss Armitage's eyes twinkled. "I'll get to that. In fact, I dislike telling the next part of the story because it is sad. The lovely little girl died very suddenly.

"Her mother was heartbroken and almost went out of her mind. Madame insisted that she and her husband move and that every object which brought back memories of the child was to be sold or given away.

"The particular object which reminded the mother of her beloved daughter was the royal coach. It was painted in gold and white and had birds and flowers carved on it. Madame felt that no one else should use it, yet she didn't want it to be destroyed. Finally she requested that it be put into a waterproof box and lowered into the bay. The whole thing was to be kept very quiet."

Everyone agreed it was a sad story indeed.

Then George said, "Evidently somebody didn't keep the secret. How did you learn about it?"

Miss Armitage said that when the child's nurse, Maud Jayson, became an old lady with a failing memory, she had told the tale but no one believed it.

"That is, no one but myself. I came across pieces of a faded torn letter in an old book which I received when the books of the little girl's mother were passed to members of the family. I happened to inherit this one."

"Did you by any chance lose one of the pieces?" Nancy asked her.

"Yes I did," Miss Armitage replied. "And it was an important part of the message. I think I lost it on the water yesterday morning. Foolishly I was carrying the letter in a small pocket."

Nancy stood up and excused herself for a minute. She went to get the paper she had found and showed it to Miss Armitage.

The woman was amazed. "This is what I lost! Where did you find it?"

Nancy told her, then said, "Miss Armitage, I've puzzled over the meaning of it. Your story is fascinating and explains the mystery."

The woman said that her reason for wanting to retrieve the child's beautiful royal coach was to present it to the Fenimore Museum.

"If the water did not get to it and the coach is intact, I think it would be a lovely addition to the historical exhibits. Thousands of people could enjoy it."

"And it would be a rare piece," Aunt Eloise added. "I doubt that there are very many like it in the world."

George asked Miss Armitage how she hoped to locate the box containing the child's coach.

"Either by feeling around with my stilts or by a long pole which I sometimes use. I thought if I located the box and could prove that the story is true, then I could hire some divers to bring it up."

Miss Armitage looked searchingly from one face to another. Finally she said, "If this mystery intrigues you, Nancy, how about solving it for me? Since you rescued me, you girls must be wonderful swimmers. You should be able to locate the coach."

Nancy accepted the challenge with alacrity, and Bess and George said they wanted to help in the search too.

"But you must promise to keep it a secret," Miss Armitage insisted.

"We promise," said the girls in unison and smilingly gave a mock salute.

The woman stood up. She wished the girls luck, then asked if one of them would drive her car home. "I still feel a little shaky," she said.

"I will," said Nancy. "Let's all go to town," she suggested. "We'll need scuba diving equipment for our search, and I can't wait to start."

Aunt Eloise begged off, saying she had letters to write.

George drove Miss Armitage's car, which the woman had parked on the road not far from Mirror Bay Bide-A-Wee. Since her home was on the opposite side of the lake, the two cars were driven through Cooperstown, then out Route 80, which ran alongside the water.

When they reached the attractive rented cottage, Bess carried the stilts inside. For the first time Miss Armitage laughed aloud.

"How foolish I've been! I think I ought to give away those stilts. To think of all the trouble I put you girls to and wasn't accomplishing a thing myself!"

"Don't worry about that," Nancy said quickly. "And please keep the stilts. Some time when you're feeling strong, I want you to give us a demonstration."

"I will if you'll all try them," Miss Armitage said. After a brief pause, she added, "By the way, you aren't far from the Farmers' Museum. That's a great place to visit. You know who's there? The Cardiff Giant."

"Who's he?" George asked.

The retired schoolteacher would not reveal any more. "You're so close now, why don't you find out for yourselves?"

"Maybe we will," Nancy replied. "But first we want to shop for scuba equipment."

The girls returned to the centre of Cooperstown in Nancy's car and parked near a restaurant. Yo was just coming out of it.

He seemed very glad to see them. Grinning, he asked, "Have you met the green man yet?"

To his surprise their answer was yes. "Really? Tell me about it," he said.

The girls related their experience and told about the man saying there was trouble at Bide-A-Wee cabin.

"It wasn't true. It was only an excuse to get us away," George said angrily. "Yo, have you any idea at all what's going on up in those woods?"

"No," the young man replied. "But I'd like to find out. To tell the truth, though, I don't think that green guy is fooling around. He wouldn't hesitate to harm any of us."

"Then," said Bess, "I for one will stay out of his reach!"

Nancy changed the subject and asked Yo where they could buy scuba equipment. He told them, then George inquired if he knew about the Cardiff Giant at the Farmers' Museum.

"Oh, yes," Yo replied. "Wait until you see that moth-eaten old Indian."

"Tell us about him," Bess urged.

Yo grinned but refused. Finally the girls left him. Nancy said that before going to the sports shop, she would like to stop at the post office up the street.

"I want to see if there are any letters for us sent to General Delivery."

Several were handed over to her. The one Nancy tore open first was from Ned Nickerson, her favourite date.

As soon as she finished reading it, Nancy exclaimed, "Girls! Listen to this!"

She read part of the letter aloud. It said, "Now I can tell you a surprise which your Aunt Eloise and I have arranged. She invited Burt, Dave, and me to come up to your cabin. We'll be there this weekend!"

"How super!" Bess cried out. "Best news I've heard in ages."

"Great!" George commented with a grin.

Burt Eddleton was a special friend of hers, and Dave Evans dated Bess.

Nancy went on, "Ned also says, 'Be sure to have a mystery waiting for us.' "

The three girls giggled. "Mystery!" Bess exclaimed. "We're full of them!"

Nancy remarked that she would give up her room, and bunk with her aunt so the three boys could use hers. "It's lucky there are three beds in it."

The girls went back to the street and walked to the shop where scuba diving equipment could be purchased. After choosing some they went to the car and set off for the Farmers' Museum on the west side of the lake.

The exhibits were housed in a huge barn and several smaller buildings. The adjoining grounds were laid out as a reproduction of a colonial village with separate offices for a lawyer, a doctor, and a printer. There also were a pharmacist's shop, a blacksmith's, a pioneer homestead, a schoolhouse, and a church.

In the huge barn the girls were intrigued by demonstrations of broom-making, spinning, and weaving. They walked all the way through the building. In a nearby shed stood a large unusual-looking vehicle.

"What's that?" Bess asked, perplexed.

When the girls drew closer, they could read a sign saying that the vehicle was a snow roller. It was horse-drawn and pulled what looked like a tremendous barrel nearly the width of an old-time country road.

George remarked, "Clearing away snow in olden

days must've really been a task. Think of how easy it is today with motorized equipment."

"Now let's go see the Cardiff Giant," Nancy suggested.

Bess pleaded, "But first I want to buy some of that old-fashioned candy."

Before Nancy and George could decide which to do, a cry rang out loud and clear in the big barn.

"Stop thief!"

·7·

Scuba Search

As the cry of "Stop thief!" was repeated, Nancy, Bess and George raced into the great barn.

At the same moment they saw the girl who resembled Nancy. She was darting in and out among the sight-seers, but Nancy caught sight of her dropping a purse into a shopping bag she carried. The girl's own bag hung over her arm.

"She's the one!" George exclaimed to the people around her, and put on a burst of speed to catch the thief.

As Nancy started to follow, she was jolted to a full stop by two hands that grabbed her shoulders from behind. She turned to face her assailant, a red-faced, angry woman.

Seizing one of Nancy's wrists in a crushing grip, she shrieked, "Here she is! She's the one! She stole my purse!"

Bess, just behind Nancy, yanked the woman's hands away.

"What do you think you're doing?" she asked, her eyes flashing. "My friend Nancy Drew is not a thief!"

By this time a crowd had gathered around the group. A guard pushed his way through to confront them.

"What's going on here?" he demanded.

"This girl stole my purse!" the woman cried out. "Arrest her! Make her give me back my money!"

"Where is the bag?" the guard asked Nancy sternly.

"I don't have it," she replied. "Evidently the thief resembles me very strongly. She got away. But a friend of mine has gone after her."

The guard looked as if he was not sure whom to believe. Bess kept insisting that Nancy had nothing to do with the theft.

At that moment George returned. "I didn't catch her," she said. "That girl jumped into a car on the road. The driver no doubt was waiting for her. It went racing off."

"What did the girl look like?" the guard asked her.

"Very much like my friend here, and she had on similar clothes," George answered.

Nancy had observed this herself, and wondered whether the thief had been shadowing her. Had she deliberately planned the theft to embarrass Nancy and also give herself a chance to get away?

To the guard, Nancy said, "You've heard the vacation hoax story, of course?" He nodded. "Well," she went on, "that girl is no doubt the same one who took this woman's purse."

The victim had been staring hard at Nancy. Now she said, "I can see the difference in the two of you. You're pretty and you have a kind face. That other girl is very hard-looking. I'm sorry I accused you."

"I'm glad we got things straightened out," Nancy replied.

The guard suggested that the woman come to the museum office and tell her story to the police, whom he would summon. The crestfallen victim followed him.

"I'm glad that's over," Bess remarked. "For a few minutes I was afraid you were going to land at police headquarters, Nancy."

"To tell the truth," her friend answered, with a little grin, "I was too."

George reminded the others that they had been on their way to look at the Cardiff Giant. "Come along!" she urged. "I want to see that moth-eaten Indian."

The girls went outdoors and hurried to the large shed beneath which the giant lay. The three girls stared at it and burst out laughing.

"That Yo and his moth-eaten Indian!" Bess said. "The only thing about this being a giant is his size. He's just carved out of wood and pretty crudely at that. He has an Indian face, though."

Nancy read a sign tacked to the wall. It explained that the Cardiff Giant had been a hoax perpetrated many, many years before. A man had carved the figure, then buried it on a farm in Cardiff, New York, to age the wood. Finally he had dug it up. The man had publicized the giant widely as having been carved in ancient times by Indians. His story caught on so well that he and a partner had travelled all over the country exhibiting their "prehistoric Indian figure".

Newspapers and various periodicals had run stories about the Cardiff Giant and the men had made thousands of dollars before the hoax was discovered.

After Bess had read the sign, she said indignantly, "Why, that faker! He was nothing but a thief!"

The girls moved off and went to buy the old-fashioned candy. After some more sightseeing they returned to the parking area.

As they drove through the exit gate, Yo was waiting for them. He wore a broad grin and called, "How did you like the withered old Indian?"

George opened the door to let Yo in, and replied, "You old fraud you! I guess I'll have to give you credit for really fooling us this time. One good hoax deserves another, I suppose."

Yo laughed and said, "What you doing this afternoon?"

"If I tell you," said Nancy, "are you going to play another joke on us?" He laughed, and she added, "We're going swimming."

They dropped him off in town. On the way home Nancy decided his mysterious smile at the dock yesterday might have indicated he liked to play jokes.

The instant the girls arrived at Bide-A-Wee, they thanked Miss Drew for her secret invitation to the boys.

Bess added, "Tell us what to do to help get ready for them and we'll start."

"Oh, tomorrow will do. Why don't we all go swimming? You can try out your scuba equipment and hunt for the child's coach."

"Great idea," Nancy agreed, "I keep wondering, if we do find it, what condition the box will be in. Maybe it has disintegrated and floated away."

"Yes," Bess added, "and the coach could be a sorry sight after lying in water for a couple of hundred years."

Nancy said if this were true Miss Armitage would be very much disappointed. "And I will too. Well, let's get started."

In a short time Aunt Eloise and her guests were swimming in Mirror Bay. The girls began hunting for the child's Russian royal coach. They found many small items in the sand, the shale and the mud, but nothing of importance until Nancy signalled the cousins to take a look at something. They swam over quickly. Their detective friend was tugging at the wheel of an object embedded in the mud.

The three girls moved it gently from side to side so as not to break the wheel off the article to which it was attached. After several seconds they unearthed a child's rusted pram and brought it to the surface. Its wicker sides were gone.

When it lay on the beach, Bess looked at it, frowning. "Don't tell me this was once a beautiful gold and white coach."

George laughed. "It's as bad as Cinderella's coach turning into a pumpkin."

Aunt Eloise looked amused. "I'd say this pram is about fifty years old, but hasn't been in the water over six months. Someone probably threw it out as junk."

The girls decided they had searched enough for this session and everyone went to dress, disappointed at another failure. They came outside again just in time to witness a gorgeous sunset across the water.

"Let's take a sunset sail," Bess proposed.

"Great idea," Nancy agreed. "Suppose you and George go out first, then I'll take Aunt Eloise while you cousins get supper!"

"That was a neat trick," George commented. "Nevertheless, I'll say okay. Come on, Bess, let's go!"

She and Bess returned in about twenty minutes, then Nancy and Aunt Eloise set off. Miss Drew worked the rudder while Nancy manned the sheet. Enough breeze had sprung up so they were able to sail almost halfway to Cooperstown. They tacked back and pulled up to the dock of Mirror Bay Bide-A-Wee.

"Something smells wonderful!" Aunt Eloise remarked. "Bess must be preparing one of her favourite recipes."

The appetizing dish turned out to be cheese soufflé served with tiny ham sandwiches, corn on the cob, and tomato salad.

After everyone had eaten, Bess called out, "Anyone for dessert?"

"I'm stuffed," George admitted.

Aunt Eloise smiled. "I'm sure whatever you have planned will be delicious. Why don't we wait until later in the evening—maybe an early midnight snack."

All agreed but Bess refused to divulge what the dessert was. A little later they went to sit on the porch. By this time it was dusk and as usual the fireflies began to flit about.

"Have you ever noticed," Aunt Eloise asked, "that most of the fireflies turn their lights on and off in unison? These are the males. The females refuse to follow this practice and flash on their little lanterns whenever they please. It's sort of a flirtation."

The girls laughed and Aunt Eloise went on to explain that entomologists say that this custom makes it easy for a male to find a mate.

Nancy spoke up. "What a perfect night for trying to find luminescent mushrooms for Karen! Why don't we climb the mountain right now and see if we can find any? They might even be in a cave. I've read that mushrooms thrive in damp caves."

George added eagerly, "I just remembered something I learned about luminescent mushrooms or some kind of fungi growing in the jungle. It seems that during wartime Japanese soldiers used to rub the palms of their hands with this phosphorescent material and could read a letter or military order by holding their hands over the sheet."

"How amazing!" Bess said.

She was not particularly keen about going on the trek because of the green man, but since her friends were making the climb she felt compelled to go along. Nancy felt no alarm and tried to reassure Bess.

The trekkers took flashlights but did not turn them on. The fireflies lighted their way. Aunt Eloise suggested that they not talk and attract attention, so the group climbed in silence, looking for the luminescent mushrooms. They saw none.

In a little while Nancy and her friends approached the area where they had encountered the green man. There was no sign of him and they heard no voice. Bess had just begun to feel secure against danger when suddenly she grabbed Nancy's arm in a gesture of fright.

·8·

Bess's Fright

QUIVERING with fear, Bess could not speak but she pointed to the girls' right. Some distance away, in the dark forest, they saw the green man enveloped in his weird green light! His face looked more ghoulish than ever. Nancy and her companions stood rooted to the spot, waiting for his next move.

Nancy was asking herself, "Does he know we're here? If so, is he hoping to scare us away? But why?"

The green light suddenly went out. The man vanished.

"He couldn't have gone far," the young detective said to herself. "I'm going to find out where he is."

She signalled the others to follow her as she made her way along swiftly but noiselessly. Everything went smoothly for about a hundred feet. Then Bess, who was reluctantly bringing up the rear, stumbled over a tree root and fell down.

Involuntarily she gave a little cry. The others stopped walking and looked back. Bess was picking herself up and waved that she was all right. Nancy hoped that if the green man had heard the sound, he might think the cry had come from some night animal.

"It did seem like an owl," she told herself.

Nancy's hopes were in vain. A few seconds later the same voice the girls had heard the evening before called out, "Who's there?"

Aunt Eloise and the others stood stock-still and did not reply. There was no further sound from the unseen man. A few seconds later Nancy decided to take a chance and go on.

George and Aunt Eloise followed, but Bess remained in one spot, paralysed with fear. Just as she made up her mind to push forward, she was suddenly grabbed from behind and a strong hand clapped over her mouth.

Bess struggled to get away from her captor. She tried to scream but could make only gurgling sounds, which her friends could not hear. Her abductor began to drag her down the mountain.

Since there had been no outcry, Bess's friends were unaware of the girl's plight. A few moments later, however, Nancy heard scraping sounds behind her. Turning to find out what was making them, she realized that Bess was not with the group.

Aunt Eloise and George looked also and together the three began to retrace their steps. Bess was not in sight. Where was she?

Nancy whispered worriedly, "I think someone has kidnapped Bess! Those scraping sounds are being made by her heels as she's dragged down the mountain!"

The searchers turned on their flashlights and hurriedly followed the sounds. The abductor stayed on the trail. In a few moments Nancy saw Bess ahead of them. A masked figure was clutching her around the arms and had a hand clapped over her mouth.

"Stop that!" Aunt Eloise shouted, running as fast as she could over the uneven ground.

At once Bess's captor dropped her, turned, and ran pell-mell down the hill. As Nancy and the others rushed towards Bess, the young detective kept wondering why the man had taken that route.

"Could he be the green man, or someone in league with him?"

There was no time for further speculation. By now the kidnapped girl was sitting up and declaring she was all right.

"But my legs are too wobbly for me to stand yet," she confessed.

"We'll carry you back to the cabin," George offered.

"I'll be all right," Bess insisted. "That guy didn't harm me. Give me a few minutes to collect my wits. I've had a pretty bad scare."

"I'll say you did," Aunt Eloise agreed. "We'll sit here for a while. When you feel like talking, tell us exactly what happened."

Nancy spoke up. "I'm sure neither the green man nor his cohorts will expect any of us to go back to that area. I'd like to sneak up to it and see if I can learn anything."

As Aunt Eloise started to object, Nancy added, "I'll be careful, really I will. It isn't far from here and you'll know where to find me if I don't return."

Miss Drew finally consented but insisted that Nancy return within ten minutes. Otherwise they would investigate.

"I'll be here," her niece promised.

Nancy turned off her flashlight and disappeared among the trees. Instead of going up the regular path and turning right, she took a shortcut directly to the area where they had seen the green man. Within a short time she was at the spot and stood still to listen. Were her ears deceiving her or had she heard voices?

"Yes, I did," she said to herself.

From somewhere nearby she could clearly detect a subdued conversation.

A man said, "I don't want people coming around here, do you understand? It's too dangerous. Sam, you're in charge of security for this project. You've got to do a better job than just looking spooky."

There was a long pause, then Sam replied, "Listen, Mike, your way would bring the police to our headquarters in no time, and you don't want that."

This remark was followed by a long silence. Nancy could not hear a sound. No lights, no men appeared from anywhere.

"I'll investigate this place in daylight," the young detective told herself. "It might be a good idea to mark the spot."

She reached up to the tall pine alongside which she was standing and broke off a good-sized piece of bark.

"That should be enough identification when I return," she decided.

Nancy quickly hurried back to her friends, who looked relieved, and excitedly whispered to them what she had learned.

"So there is something underhanded going on in this area," Bess remarked as she stood up and started trudging down the hillside. "Well, I for one refuse to come here again and I advise all of you to stay away also. Let the police solve this mystery."

The group discussed whether or not Bess's near

abduction was cause for getting in touch with the authorities that night, but after discussing it for several minutes they decided to let the incident pass temporarily.

"Let's make up our minds tomorrow morning," Aunt Eloise suggested. "I'm sure everyone is exhausted. A good night's sleep will do each of us a lot of good."

By the time they reached the cabin, Bess had recovered completely from her frightening experience and insisted they eat the dessert she had prepared. It proved to be a generous helping of wild strawberry mousse heaped in the centre of a ring of fluffy sponge cake.

"Is this ever yummy!" Nancy exclaimed. "I'm glad we waited."

Everyone slept soundly, but early the next morning there was a loud knock on the front door. Nancy and Aunt Eloise put on robes and answered the summons. Miss Drew opened the door wide to find a state trooper standing there.

"I'm Officer Duffy," he introduced himself. The trooper stared at Nancy. "Where were you last night?" he asked with a stern expression.

Nancy explained that the group in the cabin had taken a walk up the mountainside, then had gone to bed.

"Why are you asking?"

In reply he said, "Will you please come out on the porch? I can see you better here and I want to get a good look at you."

Still puzzled, Nancy did as requested. Aunt Eloise followed her. He gave the girl a searching look.

Aunt Eloise frowned. "Just what are you getting at?" she asked the trooper.

To the surprise of the Drews, the officer said to Nancy, "You cover up very well, young lady. But this time we have some proof against you that identifies you as the guilty party."

"Guilty of what?" Nancy asked in amazement.

"You know, all right. And there's no use in denying it."

With that the officer pulled a picture from his pocket, saying it had been taken the night before by an infra-red camera.

"Where?" Aunt Eloise asked.

"In our largest jewellery store," the trooper replied. "An invisible camera is set up there. Perhaps you don't know what this young lady is up to. Instead of just being a sightseer, she's been robbing jewellery stores and perpetrating other crimes."

"Nonsense!" Aunt Eloise cried.

Duffy held the photograph so that Nancy and her aunt could see it. The scene revealed the burglary in the jewellery store. A man stood there but only his back showed, so he could not be identified.

The girl with him, however, was facing the camera which had taken a very clear picture of her. Undeniably the girl in it looked like Nancy Drew!

By this time Bess and George had come outside and asked what was going on. When they were shown the picture, both of them gasped.

Bess exclaimed, "This is horrible!"

Aunt Eloise turned to the officer. "We've had other problems because of this girl. She does look a lot like Nancy, but she's someone else."

George spoke up. "Officer, I should like to point out one difference. See that mark on the jewel thief's face? It's probably a big insect bite. Look at Nancy. She doesn't have one!"

The trooper's expression softened. Was he beginning to believe that Nancy was innocent?

"That's a good point, Officer, don't you think so?" Aunt Eloise smiled. "Won't you join us for breakfast? We'd like to tell you what we know about the girl in the picture."

Trooper Duffy consented and sat down on the porch. The others went into the cabin and while Aunt Eloise prepared coffee and bacon, scrambled eggs and toast, the girls dressed. The group ate picnic-style while Bess told of her harrowing experience the evening before and the appearance of the green man. The officer pulled a notebook from his pocket and wrote down a few facts.

Nancy said to him, "Would you have time this morning to accompany me to the area we've been talking about? I can find it easily and I have an idea that possibly the girl thief may be hiding there."

The trooper nodded. "I'll be glad to go." About half an hour later he and Nancy started up the mountainside. The young detective headed for the tree from which she had torn the bark.

·9·

Bat Attack

As Nancy and Officer Duffy trudged up the mountain she told him in more detail about last night's episode and the conversation she had overhead between the two men.

"Sam and Mike?" he repeated. "As soon as I get back to headquarters I'll see if there's a combination of men with those names wanted by the police." He shook his head, adding, "Pretty slim information to start with, though."

Nancy agreed that the names were fairly common. She told him that the one called Sam evidently assumed horrible disguises to frighten people.

"Of course that's no crime in itself," the trooper reminded the young detective.

She confessed that she was more curious than frightened. "I'd like to find out where the men are staying, what they're doing, and why they are scaring people away from the area."

Duffy smiled at her. He had completely lost his severe attitude. "You'll find out," he predicted.

A little while later they reached the tree from which Nancy had pulled a piece of bark and looked all around. There was no sign of a cabin, cave, or other type of shelter.

"It's just possible," the officer said, "that Sam and Mike are staying in Cooperstown or some other place nearby, and come up here only occasionally."

Duffy thought they might be scientists studying the flora of the mountainside. "As far-fetched as it may seem, it's possible they have some experiment set up and don't want it disturbed or known to anyone yet, even the police. But they sure use a strange method to scare away curious people."

Nancy said nothing, but she could not forget Mike's retort about something bringing the police there and that was what the men did not want. If the project were legal, there was certainly no harm in the authorities knowing about it.

She and the trooper walked around the area looking for possible traps, cages, miniature greenhouses, and boxes in which plants might be growing. They found none and Duffy said he must leave. He led the way to the foot of the hill.

"I'll continue to track down that girl who looks like you," he said as the two reached his car which he had parked above Bide-A-Wee.

"If you capture her," said Nancy, "I'd like to talk to her."

"I'll pass along word to the Cooperstown Village Police," Duffy promised. "That's probably where she'll be held." He handed Nancy a slip of paper. "If you have any further need for help, call me at this number."

"Thank you. I will," she said as they parted.

During Nancy's descent to her aunt's cabin, she thought about the mysterious girl. Though apparently only a few years older than Nancy, she was already guilty of some grave offences against the law.

"How much happier she'd be if she used her brains for some good cause!"

As Nancy walked up on the front porch, Aunt Eloise and the other girls plied her with questions about her trip up the mountain. She reported everything, including Officer Duffy's theory about what Sam and Mike might be doing.

"Do you agree with him?" Miss Drew asked her niece.

Nancy shook her head. "I'm sure there's some connection between that girl who looks like me and those two men. They may be scientists, but I still think they're up to something crooked."

"I agree," George said.

Nancy was determined to get to the bottom of the mystery, particularly since she might be accused each time the girl broke the law. No doubt her double was using the resemblance to her own advantage. The situation might become more difficult for Nancy to deny the charges.

Bess said, "Let's forget those people and go scuba diving. I want to hunt for that child's royal coach. It intrigues me more than thinking of the man who tried to kidnap me."

Aunt Eloise laughed. "I don't blame you. Where are you going to look now? Haven't you about exhausted this whole area?"

"I have an idea," George spoke up. "I saw an underwater metal detector in one of the kitchen cabinets. Let's take that down with us."

Within minutes Aunt Eloise was in her swimsuit and the three girls had on their scuba diving equipment. The searchers had barely started working with the detector when it began to click noisily. The girls were not in deep water and it was easy to dig into the shale and sand at the spot with their bare hands.

Almost at once each of the girls found a coin, then another, and another. Someone either on the shore or in a boat had dropped a lot of them in the water. The coins were brought to the surface and to everyone's delight they proved to be very old.

"What a discovery!" Aunt Eloise exclaimed.

The coins were of English origin and all bore early eighteenth-century dates.

Bess looked at them and remarked, "These must be worth a fortune! Let's shine them up so we can see better just what's engraved on them."

Aunt Eloise offered to do it and the girls went back to their metal detection search. Unfortunately they had no luck and finally rose to the surface and returned to the cabin.

"I'll dress to go into the village," Nancy announced. "How about all of you coming with me?"

"Any special reason?"

"Yes, two. If the coins we found are valuable, they shouldn't be left here, especially with thieves in the neighbourhood."

"You're right," said Aunt Eloise. "In this state, money that's found has to be turned over to the police within ten days. They hold it for a while. If no one claims the treasure-trove within a predetermined time, the finder keeps it. I suggest that right now we put the coins in a safe-deposit box at the bank."

Nancy nodded. "I'll phone Officer Duffy and ask him which police headquarters to report this to."

The others agreed to the arrangement, then Nancy said, "My other reason for going to the village is to find Yo. I want to ask him if he knows of any caves up on the mountain where people may be in hiding—one that the trooper and I might have missed."

"They're both good ideas," Aunt Eloise remarked. "Also, Yo may know of some place where Karen could find her luminescent fungi."

George added, "If he knows of one, why don't we get him to go along with us? Then we can tell Karen where it is."

When they reached Cooperstown, Aunt Eloise and the girls went directly to the bank, which fortunately was still open. Miss Drew arranged to rent a safe-deposit box, then inquired if there was anyone at the bank who was an expert on old coins.

"Yes," the officer answered. "One of our cashiers."

Aunt Eloise told what she had with her and an attractive young man was brought over. Miss Drew showed him the collection.

After looking at a few of the coins, he became excited. "Where did you find these?" he asked.

Miss Drew explained that her niece and two other girls had retrieved them from the bottom of the bay.

"They're very valuable," the young man said. "What do you plan to do with this treasure? I know several people who might be interested."

Aunt Eloise turned towards the girls. "You found them. What do you say?"

Nancy replied, "If it turns out we may keep the money, I'd like to give the collection to the historical museum here."

The young man beamed. "It would be a marvellous

gift. Would you like me to speak to the people there?"

"Not yet," Nancy said. "In the meantime we'll put the coins in the box, and let you know when we can show them."

"Very good," the cashier said and went back to his work.

After the old money was put away and the key given to Aunt Eloise, Nancy and the others drove to the dock. Yo was there and came to greet the girls.

"How's the mystery business coming?" he asked with a grin.

"Kind of slow," Nancy replied. "We're here to ask you a question. Have you ever seen a cave where thieves might hang out up on the mountain?"

"I sure have," the young man answered. "It's not Natty Bumppo's cave, though—too many campers and sightseers go there. You know he was the scout in Cooper's famous *Leatherstocking Tales*.

"The cave I'm thinking of is way up in the rough part of the woods. So you figure some thieves are hiding out there?"

Nancy decided to be noncommittal. "We'd like to find out one way or the other."

Yo gave her a searching look. "Do you think that green man is a crook?"

Nancy shrugged. "A State Police officer thinks he might be a scientist. Yo, could you show us the cave real soon?"

"How about late this afternoon?" he asked.

"Great," Nancy replied. "We'll be waiting for you."

"I'll be at your place after work."

When it was time to dress for the climb, Bess refused to go. Nancy and George put on their sturdiest long-sleeved shirts and dungarees. They wore hiking shoes and tied scarves around their hair.

Yo arrived about five o'clock and the three set off up the mountain. Each carried a flashlight in case they stayed until dark.

Yo did not follow the trail which the girls now knew so well. Instead, he led them through a tangle of vines and bushes among the trees. It was very rocky in places and all of them slipped and slid at times. Finally Yo said they were nearing the spot.

"We'd better go quietly," he whispered.

The three crept forward. There was not a sound from the cave.

"I guess it's safe to enter," Yo told the girls.

The cave was well sequestered. It was deep in the mountainside and the entrance was partially but effectively screened with vines.

As the three searchers stepped inside, they could see the far end of the underground cavern. It was glowing like a neon light.

The girls hurried forward, but before they could advance more than a few feet, there was a sudden sound of wings and loud squeaking. The next moment hundreds of bats came swooping down in their direction!

The searchers turned and fled.

The mouse-like flying mammals, once they were outside, were blinded by the sunlight. The little brown creatures banged into the trees and some fell to the ground, stunned. But soon most of them recovered and by instinct returned to the cave and hung upside down on the ceiling.

"I guess that ends our going in," George remarked.

"Not at all," Yo replied. "Now that the bats have

made our acquaintance and are no longer afraid of us, they won't bother us any more. To prove it to you, I'll go in first."

Yo was right. The bats did not move from their roosting place and the girls followed Yo inside. Now they could see that the cave was dimly lit by whatever was at its far end.

When they drew closer, Nancy exclaimed, "Giant luminescent mushrooms!"

"Don't try to eat them," Yo warned. "Not unless you want to end up in the hospital."

"We just solved a puzzle for someone," George told Yo. "A girl we met is hunting for luminescent fungi and here they are! We'll have to bring her up here."

"Why don't we tear one of these mushrooms from the wall and take it to her?" Nancy suggested.

"Here's my pocketknife," Yo offered, removing it from a pocket.

Nancy pulled the scarf from her head. Then, while she held it under the mushroom, he deftly removed the fungus from the wall.

"Karen will love this," she remarked. The scarf was tied and Nancy swung it over her shoulder like a little knapsack.

George asked Yo if the place he had seen the green man was near here.

"Oh no," he replied. "It was way over on the other side of the trail."

"One thing I'm sure of," Nancy said as they started back towards the entrance, "this is not a thieves' hangout. The bats would have chased them away and there's no evidence of anyone's having lived here."

"Right," Yo agreed. "Now I'll take you to what I

think is the green man's place if you like."

"Please do," Nancy replied.

When they neared the exit of the bat cave, the hikers could see that it was nearly dusk. They would need their flashlights.

Before leaving, George said, "What is this cave made of?"

She put her hand on the wall to feel the rocks. The next moment she cried out, "I've been bitten!"

Nancy and Yo turned just in time to see a giant worm-like creature on George's arm. Quickly Yo knocked it to the floor of the cave and stepped on it.

At the same time he exclaimed, "It's a poisonous centipede! *Very* poisonous!"

·10·

Footprint Lesson

As Yo made the horrifying announcement, he took George by the hand and yanked her quickly outside the cave. Even in the waning light, they could all see the puncture in the girl's forearm.

Instantly Yo leaned down and put his lips over the wound. He began to suck the poison from it, stopped to spit out the deadly fluid, then started over again. Not a word was said by Nancy and George, but they watched intently.

"That's enough," the young man said presently, and straightened up. "But don't move!"

George was too frightened to do anything but obey. Nancy asked, "Is there any way I can help?"

"Yes," Yo replied. "Help me tear off some of this wild-grape vine and strip off the leaves."

Within seconds the two had long streamers of it. Yo began to fashion a tourniquet around George's arm just above the wound. He directed Nancy to put another directly below it.

When this was accomplished, he warned George, "Be very quiet."

She stood stock-still and watched his next move. Beaming a flashlight, he searched for a small sharp stone. He cleaned it off very thoroughly on one of the grape leaves. Then he rubbed it up and down over the surface of George's uninjured arm.

To Nancy the procedure looked like hocus-pocus and she wondered, now that the danger to George was probably over, if Yo were just being silly.

She soon found out, however, that he was serious. Using the sharp edge of the stone very deftly, he made a small crisscross cut over the wound. Blood began to flow from it.

He explained, "Any poison left in the arm should drain out now. But you must still keep quiet, George. Anyone who has been bitten or stung should move as little and as slowly as possible so the heartbeat will not be stimulated."

The three sat down and remained quiet. Nancy asked Yo where he had learned how to take care of this type of puncture.

The young man smiled. "From an old Indian over in Cherry Valley. By the way, the Indians in this territory knew a great deal about how to take care of wounds and even do minor surgery. They also knew how to use healing herbs that grow around here."

As Yo removed the tourniquet, George asked him, "Was rubbing the stone over my skin some kind of magic?"

"Oh no," Yo answered. "I cleaned the stone as thoroughly as I could without water or chemicals. According to the old Indian, if there were any germs on it when I made the cut, they would be your own."

Both girls looked at Yo with new respect. He was a puzzling person. George said to him, "You saved my life. I thank you very much."

As the young man flushed in embarrassment at the praise, she added with a grin, "I suppose I'm full of germs, but I never thought of looking on my arm for them."

Nancy and Yo laughed.

"George," he said, "if you feel like walking, perhaps we'd better go. It's getting dark."

"I feel fine now, thanks to you," George assured him.

With the aid of the flashlights, the trio moved forward. Nancy begged that they not descend the mountainside over such rough ground.

"Can't we head for the trail and go back that way?"

"Sure," Yo replied, and led the way.

The trek seemed long and the undergrowth was almost impassable. George declared it was positively a jungle. After a while they came to the trail, but instead of turning down, Nancy stopped short.

"Do you hear something?" George asked her.

"No, but look at the ground. I see a very clear shoe print."

Her two companions stared at the mark made by a man's shoe. Nancy beamed her flashlight around, trying to pick up a print of the person's other shoe.

"There it is!" she said.

She leaned down and studied it intently. "If this belongs to either Sam or Mike, his right foot turns out. His left doesn't."

George added, "He walks a little unevenly and puts more weight on his right heel."

Yo stared at the two girls. "Are you detectives?" he asked.

They did not answer, but Nancy crossed the trail and began searching in the woods beyond. But the undergrowth was so thick that shoe prints were impossible to detect.

Again Yo asked if the two girls were detectives. They smiled and Nancy said, "We like mysteries."

She and George went on searching. Presently Nancy said, "The man is tall. He has a long stride."

Moments later the girls spied a different set of shoe prints. Nancy remarked, "These were made by hiking boots that probably look the worse for wear."

"How do you know that?" Yo asked, following the girls.

"You can tell by the unevenness. The man is shorter than the other one and walks straight ahead. But I'd say he makes a funny little ball-like motion with his right foot which will wear out the sole rather quickly."

Yo began to laugh quietly. "I suppose, Mrs Sherlock Holmes, that you can tell me how old each man is, and if he is a crook."

Nancy confessed that she could not possibly tell from the shoe print whether either man was a crook but she would guess from the marks that both men were in top condition and walked rather quickly.

"I judge they're in their late thirties or early forties."

Yo remarked that the girls were certainly wonders. He reminded them they had all planned to go home down the trail.

"That's right," Nancy admitted. "And, George, we should get you back to the cabin to rest."

Again George declared she felt all right and was eager to go on following the prints, so they pushed forward. Some distance ahead they came to a darkened lean-to almost covered with growth. When the girls flashed their lights inside, they found it empty.

The shoe prints ended here. Nancy was puzzled. The two men hikers could not have gone off in the air. How did they get away without leaving any marks?

Yo came up with a suggestion. "Maybe from here on, the men used the old Indian method of sweeping away their footprints with a branch with leaves."

"That's a good guess," Nancy told him. "You're probably right."

"Maybe I can qualify as a detective's assistant," the young man said, laughing.

"Could be," George agreed.

Nancy had bent down to pick up something her flashlight had revealed inside the lean-to. Then she grasped a second object.

"What are they?" George asked.

Nancy spread them on the palm of her hand and held it out.

"Bobbie pins!" George exclaimed. "A girl has been here. But why didn't she leave any footprints?"

Nancy said that she might have, but that as Yo had suggested, the marks could have been brushed away.

Yo was intrigued. "Do you think she could have been the girl who looks like you, Nancy?"

"Yes. You saw her going into the woods, so these might be hers. I think I'll leave them. She may come back here and could be captured!"

The girls found no more clues, and followed Yo to the trail. It was very dark by the time they said goodbye to him and entered the cabin.

"Thank goodness you're back," said Bess. "Why, George, what ever happened to you?" Bess had noticed the mark on her cousin's arm.

"Oh, a little confrontation between me and a poisonous centipede."

"What!" Bess cried. "Why, he might have killed you!" When she and Miss Drew were told the story, they too praised Yo for his quick action.

Aunt Eloise noticed Nancy's scarf. "What are you carrying in there?"

Nancy untied her bundle and turned off the lights. The luminescent mushroom glowed brightly.

"How marvellous!" Bess remarked. "What are you going to do with it?"

"Take it to Karen," Nancy replied. She looked at her wrist watch. "It's still early. Bess, let's drive over to her camp now and present it."

Bess was eager to go, so the two girls set off in Nancy's car. When they reached Karen's camp, the instructor was just coming back to her tent. She greeted the girls warmly.

When Nancy presented her gift, Karen was thrilled. "*Where* did you find this?"

Nancy told her and gave Karen directions to the cave. "But be careful. There are bats and poisonous centipedes in the place."

Karen's eyes grew large. "Oh, I'd hate to face them! I'll think twice about going there. But thanks a million for everything. This was a wonderful find."

At that moment her young campers began to arrive so Nancy and Bess said good night and headed home.

Early the following morning the girls spent an hour cleaning and straightening the cabin in preparation for the boys' arrival. Nancy moved into her aunt's bedroom and changed the sheets and pillowcase on the bed she had used.

Aunt Eloise had gone to pick some wild flowers and set them on the combination living-dining room table.

"What time are the boys getting in?" George asked.

"Between five and five-thirty, I believe," Nancy told her.

The group went out to the porch to sit down and rest before going swimming. They heard footsteps on the path leading to the cabin and soon saw Miss Armitage approaching.

"Good morning! Good morning!" she said cheerily. "How is everything going?"

"We used scuba diving equipment a couple of times," Nancy replied, "and really are hunting hard for the child's coach. So far there hasn't been a clue, but yesterday we did make a real find." She told the woman about the valuable old coins.

"That's wonderful," Miss Armitage said. "Do you plan to scuba dive this morning? I came down here hoping to watch you. I thought maybe I might bring you luck."

"Yes, we're going very soon," George spoke up. "In fact, I think I'll get ready now."

Nancy and Bess followed her, and in a little while they were ready to make another search for the buried coach. Nancy held the metal detector and the three friends disappeared under the water. Miss Armitage and Aunt Eloise watched intently.

"They're wonderful, brave girls," the visitor stated.

"Yes, they are," Miss Drew agreed, "but sometimes Nancy becomes too enthusiastic and runs into danger."

Within minutes Nancy rose to the surface and swam to the dock. "Come here and get a treasure!" she exclaimed, setting an object on the dock.

The object proved to be a child's metal piggy bank that rattled with coins. Both women laughed heartily as they returned to the porch. Miss Drew went inside to make some coffee. A minute later she heard Miss Armitage give a blood-curdling scream.

"What could have happened?" Aunt Eloise asked herself in alarm as she rushed to the porch.

·11·

Valentine Clue

"WHAT'S the matter?" Aunt Eloise cried out when she reached the porch.

Miss Armitage pointed to a fast-disappearing motor-boat. "That driver nearly killed Bess!"

She explained that Bess had just surfaced when the boat raced past. Either the girl in the boat had not seen Bess or had deliberately tried to hit her!

"Where is Bess now?" Miss Drew asked anxiously.

"Bess saw the boat heading for her and dived. There she is!" Miss Armitage added as Bess once more appeared on the surface.

This time she did not dive again but swam towards the dock and pulled herself up. Miss Armitage and Aunt Eloise rushed down to her.

"Are you all right?" they both inquired as she took off her mask.

"Yes," Bess replied rather weakly. "But that boat sure gave me a scare."

Nancy and George came up a few seconds later and were told what had happened. Nancy asked Miss Armitage to describe the boat and the driver.

"The boat was the *Water Witch* and it was a nice-looking speedboat," the woman replied.

"*Witch* is a good name for it," George remarked.

Miss Armitage studied Nancy and then said, "The girl in the boat looked a lot like you, only she had a hard face."

Bess, George, and the Drews glanced knowingly at one another. Finally Nancy said, "We keep hearing about that girl. Actually she's wanted by the police. You heard about the vacation hoax, didn't you?"

Miss Armitage nodded. Nancy went on, "She's the one responsible for cheating all those people. We were told she has a man partner who probably lives in New York City."

Miss Armitage asked, "What is she doing up here? If the police are looking for her, it seems to me she's pretty brazen to be out on the lake and to come so close to the person who resembles her. It's my guess, Nancy, that she was trying to hurt you but almost hit Bess instead."

The girls decided not to do any more scuba diving until after the boys arrived. "We'll continue working on your mystery tomorrow," Nancy assured the woman as she drank the coffee Aunt Eloise had brought out.

A short time later the caller got up to leave. After she had gone, the others again discussed the boat episode. Nancy declared she was going to find out the name of the person who had piloted it.

Bess interrupted. "Let's go see the sights this afternoon. It's a lot safer than working on a mystery."

Aunt Eloise begged off, saying she had been to all the museums the summer before. "One you'll love is the Toy Museum. It's on the west side of the lake and a good distance from town."

The girls thought it sounded interesting, and as soon as lunch was over, decided to drive there. They went to

Cooperstown, then took Route 80 towards Springfield Centre. At last they came to the old farmhouse and barn which were used as a toy museum.

Nancy parked and the girls went inside the house. They paid their admission, then a tall, slender, affable man introduced himself as the owner and said he would take them on a tour of the place.

"You understand," he said, "that nearly everything here is very old. The toys and other pieces were gathered from this general area and are anywhere from fifty to two hundred years old."

First they came to the dolls. Bess declared she had never seen so many altogether. There were men, women, boy and girl dolls made of various materials, and dressed in every imaginable kind of costume.

Some had very pretty faces and lovely lace or embroidered dresses. Most of the boy dolls wore sailor hats and tight-fitting clothes. The amusing ones had grotesque faces, others were happy clowns. Also on display were many kinds of buggies and other vehicles in which children had given their dolls rides.

Bess whispered to Nancy and George, "I don't see anything as beautiful as the child's Russian coach must be."

Another room contained mechanical toys, and another a complete antique train set which whizzed round corners and under mountains.

Finally they came to the room containing old books. The trio was amused by pictures of little girls in pantaloons with disproportionate bodies. Bess mentioned this to the owner.

He laughed. "Nobody knows the reason for this strange period in art. All old-time pictures of children were the same. The bodies always look stumpy and the head much too large. You'll even find this to be true in fine antique gallery paintings, even those depicting angels."

While he was speaking, Nancy was looking up at a shelf on which stood a row of valentines. They looked old and were very fancy with their imitation lace paper covers and pictures of hearts and cupids.

Suddenly something special about one valentine caught Nancy's eye. In the elaborate scroll-work on the cover she could detect a name. It looked like Maud Jayson.

Excited, Nancy asked the owner if he would mind getting it down to let her see it more closely. She nudged Bess and George and traced the name when the man was not looking.

The cousins were startled. Could this be the same Maud Jayson involved in the mystery of the missing child's royal coach?

Nancy carefully opened the letter-type valentine. Inside, written in precise, old-fashioned script was a message evidently intended for Maud Jayson. It read:

> Ever faithful to thee
> And the memory of the little lass
> Her lovely pony coach
> Lying 'neath the Glimmerglass
> NOE
> 5   R

The girls could hardly refrain from exclaiming aloud. Here was a wonderful clue to the mystery they were trying to solve!

As nonchalantly as she could, Nancy asked the owner, "Is this for sale?"

The man smiled. "Not really. I need it for my museum. But," he added with a grin, "if somebody offered me a really good price for the valentine, I might sell it." His eyes twinkled as he waited for an answer.

"I don't know what to offer you but I'd like very much to have it," Nancy told him, naming a price.

The owner replied, "It's worth much more than that."

Nancy made a second bid. She was trying to guess how much money the three girls had among them.

"Tell you what, young lady," he said. "Add another ten and we'll call it a sale."

Nancy was relieved. She had only a little more than that with her! The amount seemed like a lot of money to pay for one valentine. Still she was sure the clue it contained about the child's royal coach was well worth the price.

"I'll take it," she said.

As soon as the valentine was wrapped, the three girls thanked the owner for the tour and said they must go.

"Oh, I have lots more to show you," the man said, surprised.

Nancy promised they would all come back sometime but right now they had an important errand to do and must leave.

When they were in the car, Bess asked, "What's on your mind Nancy?"

"To hurry to Miss Armitage's and show her this valentine. Maybe she can decipher the code message. I'm intrigued by the N and the E with the backward C in between."

When they reached her home, Miss Armitage greeted the girls warmly.

"Wait until you see what Nancy has to show you!" Bess exclaimed.

As soon as Miss Armitage saw the valentine, tears came into her eyes. Nancy asked her if she could translate the letters and number on it.

The woman studied them a few minutes, then said, "I can't help you with the names on the left, but I'm sure the letter R stands for Robert. He was the houseman for the Russian lady whose little girl died.

"Robert was very much in love with Maud Jayson and asked her over and over to marry him but she always refused. We don't know why. Neither of them ever married."

Miss Armitage and the girls studied the other symbols for nearly half an hour, making many guesses but reaching no conclusions.

Bess looked at her watch. "We must go!" she exclaimed. "The boys will be arriving any time!"

Nancy said, "Miss Armitage, I suppose this valentine should become your property, but may I keep it for a while to see if I can figure out these other symbols? I'm sure there's a clue in it that will help us find the child's coach."

"Please take it," the woman said. "And good luck."

The girls had barely reached Bide-A-Wee, washed their hands, and combed their hair when the weekend visitors arrived. Ned, tall and attractive-looking, was first. Behind him was Dave, blond and with a rangy build. Behind him came Burt, blond, short and husky. Following him was a very handsome, distinguished-looking man about Aunt Eloise's age.

The three boys kissed their friends and also Aunt Eloise, whom they knew well.

Then Burt turned and said, "Miss Drew, I'd like to present my uncle, Professor Matthew Bronson, B.S., M.A., Ph.D. He's going to be teaching chemistry at Emerson this year. Uncle Matt, meet Nancy Drew and Bess Marvin and George Fayne."

The professor smiled broadly, shook hands with everyone, and said, "Burt has given me a long frightening title. Please forget I'm a professor and call me Matt."

He carried a suitcase with him so Aunt Eloise and the girls assumed he planned to stay. As if reading their thoughts, he said:

"The boys insisted that I come down and meet you. I know you're crowded here so later I'll go back into Cooperstown to a hotel."

Aunt Eloise gave him a big smile. "Matt, you'll do nothing of the sort. We have this extra cot on the porch. It can either be moved into the boys' room or you can sleep out here if you wish. In any case, do stay."

"I'd enjoy the fresh air," the professor replied. "And how beautiful the view is! The bay is like a mirror."

Miss Drew nodded. "We like to eat out here and watch the changing scenes on the water. I'm sure you'll enjoy them too."

"I couldn't refuse such a hospitable invitation," Matt said, giving his hostess a warm, friendly look which made Miss Drew blush.

Bess turned to look at Nancy and George. They knew she was thinking, "Is a romance coming up?"

·12·

Firefly Secrets

NANCY and George grinned at Bess's implication of a romance between Miss Drew and the professor. Romance or not, it was pretty thoughtful of the boys to supply a companion for Aunt Eloise. Then she would never be left alone when the three couples went off together. Both Aunt Eloise and Matt looked quite pleased with the arrangement.

The professor proved to be a delightful conversationalist and revealed that he had made a study of the early days in New York State when it was settled by the Dutch.

"I came across many amusing and puzzling items," he said. "It seems that at the time every man was his own dictionary. For instance, the word *wheat* was spelled wett—weat—wheate—weate—whitt—whaet—witt and weett!"

"Tell us more," Nancy begged.

"I'll write out something," Matt said. "See if you can translate the item which appeared in a ledger." He wrote: I peare shouse meade for your wife.

Nancy studied the words a moment, then replied, "One pair shoes made for your wife."

"Right," Matt said.

Aunt Eloise and the girls went to prepare dinner. It was served on the porch. As they ate, Ned asked Nancy, "What's new? Do you have a mystery that we fellows can help solve?"

"You mean mysteries," Bess replied. "One is nice and kind of fun even if an enemy of ours tried to run over me with a motor-boat."

"What!" Dave exclaimed.

An account of Bess's near accident was given. The discovery of the old coins was related next, and the finding of the piggy bank brought a good laugh.

"Was anything in it?" Burt inquired.

"Yes. We're pretty sure it's full of pennies," George answered. "We haven't tried yet to open it. Maybe they are old, old pennies and probably worth a good bit of money."

George went to get the piggy bank and it was prised open with a screwdriver. There were several dollars' worth of pennies, but none of them was old enough to have any extra value.

The girls then told the visitors about the child's Russian coach reported by Miss Armitage to be at the bottom of the bay.

"Promise you won't divulge any of this," George ended.

Burt smiled. "Any of what?" he asked in mock confusion.

Dave and Ned chimed in, "Did you reveal a secret?"

After a moment of light-hearted teasing from the boys, Nancy spoke up. "We want you to help us hunt for it."

Dave remarked, "The search really sounds intriguing."

"It looks," said Ned, smiling, "as if we just got here in time. Any more mysteries?"

Bess laughed. "We could keep you up all night telling everything we've heard and suspect and found out and haven't found out."

The episodes on the mountainside involving the luminescent green man, his strange disappearances, and the glowing mushrooms in the cave with the poisonous centipede were related.

"George!" exclaimed Burt. "What a terrible experience!"

Matt had been silent up to this point but now he said, "I never heard of so many things happening in such a short time to people on vacation. I myself am interested in bio-luminescence of fungi and insects. In fact, in my chemistry courses I've done some special work on it."

Bess said, "You'll have to meet Karen, an instructor at a camp near here. She's a botany student and is studying about luminescent fungi. You could probably give her a lot of pointers on the subject."

Burt interrupted. "Now don't you be making any dates for Uncle Matt. He's here to have a good time and to forget chemistry for a while."

Matt Bronson looked at his nephew and laughed. "When one is intensely interested in a subject, he never becomes tired of it, even on a vacation," he said. "Look at Nancy, for instance. I suppose she was invited up here just to have fun, and now she's involved in all these mysteries."

The conversation was interrupted by a call from the dock. "Hello! Anybody home?"

"I think that's Yo," Nancy explained. "His full name is Johann Bradley but everyone calls him Yo."

She turned towards the water and shouted down, "Is that you, Yo?"

"Yes."

"Come on up."

When the pudgy young man arrived, he was introduced to the newcomers and shook hands with each of them. Then he said, "Nancy, I have a clue for you."

"Wonderful. What is it?"

Yo said he had seen the girl who resembled her getting on a bus in Cooperstown. It was going to New York City.

"That *is* news," Nancy agreed.

Yo grinned. "I guess she's gone for good. Bet you're glad of that."

"If it's true, of course, I'm glad," she answered. "But she might come back."

Nancy was wondering if the mysterious girl were mixed up in another vacation hoax. She asked Yo if he knew anything about a boat named the *Water Witch*.

"I've seen it at a Cooperstown dock," he said. "I believe it's a private one."

When he was told that the girl who resembled Nancy had been piloting the boat and almost hit Bess, Yo offered to find out who owned it.

He abruptly changed the subject and said to Matt Bronson, "Have you ever been up in this neck of the woods before?"

"No I haven't. I understand it's very interesting historically."

Yo declared it was more than that. "It's ghost country!"

"Really?" Matt said, a twinkle in his eye.

Yo was serious. "You don't believe me? Well, I'll tell

you a story that's absolutely true."

The others listened intently as Yo began his ghostly tale. "Not far from here on a certain night a long time ago a man and his wife were riding in a one-horse carriage. It was a lonely road and they were pretty far from town. Both of them became very weary. Presently they saw a light in a house a short distance ahead and the man said, 'Perhaps these people will let us have lodging for the night.'

"They rode up to the front door, which was opened by a nice elderly couple. The travellers explained their situation and asked if they might stay overnight. The farmer said, 'Yes, indeed.' He directed the man to unhitch his horse and put him in an empty stall of the barn. He did this, then the travellers went into the house.

"They were shown to a plain but comfortable bedroom upstairs and soon were sound asleep. They woke up early the next morning and decided not to bother their host and hostess but to slip away. They hitched up their horse and drove into town. People there asked where they had spent the night.

"When the travellers told them, everyone stared in amazement and fear. 'What was so strange about that?' the man asked.

"The reply was that the house had burned down many years before.

" 'But we did sleep there,' the couple insisted and could not be talked out of it. Finally one of the men in town said he would drive back with the couple and prove it to them. They went all the way to the farm and sure enough the house had burned to the ground."

As Yo stopped speaking, Ned remarked, "And

there's something else to the story. Before the travellers left the farm that next morning, the man put a fifty-cent piece on a marble-top table in the hall. When the couple returned, they could hardly believe their eyes. On the marble top, which was the only part left of the table, lay the fifty-cent piece!"

Yo's eyes opened wide. "How'd you know that?" he asked.

For an answer Ned merely grinned. Yo asked no more questions. Announcing he must leave, he stood up and said goodbye to everyone. A few minutes later he was roaring off in his outboard motor-boat.

Nancy said to Ned, "You'd heard that ghost story before."

"Yes, but you'd never guess where. In connection with my psychology course at Emerson this past year. We took up the study of ghosts. Scholars of this subject declare that all these stories are merely folklore."

Night had come on by this time and the fireflies seemed to be everywhere. Aunt Eloise remarked how much they fascinated her and the various things she had learned about them.

"But I still don't understand what gives them power to light up and then turn off."

Matt smiled. "Perhaps I can help you if you can stand some big words. First of all, a firefly is a beetle and the term lightning bug is probably more appropriate than firefly. Five different chemicals, among them luciferin, are bound together in the abdomen of the beetle. Nerve stimulations release a sixth chemical which breaks up the bond of five. This reaction produces the light. A few seconds later a seventh chemical destroys the sixth one and the light goes out.

"Scientists are extremely interested in cold light which beetles can produce—but man hasn't yet been able to! Many deep-sea fish light up, also, and some shrimp, jellyfish, worms, and molluscs."

Aunt Eloise asked, "Do many scientists use fireflies in their work?"

"Yes, in their search for the magic formula of cold heat. I've been working on this problem, not with fireflies or anything else living, but with the chemicals which cause the phenomenon. So far I haven't had much luck, but this year I'm going to concentrate solely on this subject."

As Matt paused, the stillness was suddenly shattered by a wild cry on the hillside above the cabin. Then came the sounds of a body hurtling down the hillside.

·13·

The Vanishing Spook

EVERYBODY rushed from the porch of the cottage and hurried up the hill. On a level area about halfway to the road lay a young woman.

"You're hurt!" Aunt Eloise exclaimed. "We'll carry you to our cabin."

"No, no," the girl objected. "I got very scared and ran and lost my balance." She sat up. "I'm all right, really I am."

Despite what she said, the stranger was pale and trembling. She was covered with dust and her shoulder-length hair was tousled.

"Can we take you some place?" Ned spoke up.

The girl shook her head. "Just help me to the road and please stay until my boy friend comes. He's going to pick me up. I was early getting off my job at the motel so I started walking towards Cooperstown. I'm Mary Storr."

The boys assisted the young woman to her feet while the girls brushed off her clothes. Bess pulled a small comb from her pocket and smoothed the girl's lovely curly brown hair. Nancy had taken some tissues from a pocket and helped Mary wipe the dirt from her face.

"My boy friend won't know me," Mary said ruefully.

"What frightened you?" George asked.

A shiver ran through Mary's body. "A ghost that came out of the woods. You know, there are spooks around this area. I never heard of a green one, though."

"The green man!" Bess exclaimed. "We've seen him too."

Mary Storr looked startled. "Then I wasn't dreaming? People tell me that there are no such things as ghosts. I didn't want to say anything for fear you'd laugh at me."

"That green man is no laughing matter," Bess declared.

"The figure wasn't really green," Mary told them. "It was all in white with a hood. But a funny green light would glow around it for a few seconds, then go off."

"Wow! I don't blame you for being frightened," Dave spoke up. "Where'd the guy go?"

Mary Storr said she did not know. "When this white thing started waving its arms towards me like somebody casting a spell, I started to run. I was getting ahead of him, but turned to look back. That's when I stumbled on something near your path and lost my balance. I started rolling down the hill."

By this time the group had reached the road, which was dark. There was no sign of the strange figure.

"Thank goodness he's gone," she said. "And thank you all very much for bringing me up here. You can bet I'll never walk in this area alone again."

As she spoke, headlights appeared in the distance and in a couple of minutes a young man drew up alongside the group. Mary excitedly explained to him why she and the others were there.

Her boy friend looked worried. "Thanks, folks," he said. "Mary, hop in here and let's get away from this place. I don't like spooks."

After they had gone, Ned said, "How about hiking up the mountain to find this weird creature?"

Aunt Eloise decided to go back to the cabin and clear away the dinner dishes. Matt said he would help her. The six young people were trudging up the hill on the opposite side of the road when Nancy remarked that they should have brought flashlights.

"I'll go back and get a few," Burt offered.

The others waited for him. When he returned he had lights for each couple. As they neared the place where the girls had seen the green man previously, George said she wondered if he were the same person who had frightened Mary Storr.

"If so, he has a variety of costumes," Dave commented.

"I believe," said Nancy, "that he's the same person using various disguises." She added that her conclusion was based on the conversation she overheard between Sam and Mike.

"So the ghost is a sorcerer too," Ned said. "We'd better watch our step. By the way, I've heard that when a sorcerer bewitches a person, he in turn can pass the witchery on to someone else without the other one knowing it."

George laughed. "You mean that Mary Storr might have passed the sorcery along to one of us here?"

"Could be," Ned teased. "When we get back we might even find Aunt Eloise and Matt turned into stone statues!"

Nancy was grinning broadly. "Ned," she said, "is

this part of what you learned in your folklore lessons?"

"You've guessed it," he said, chuckling.

As they trekked up the mountain, it was not necessary for the young people to turn on the flashlights.
With their vision accustomed to the darkness and the
twinkling of the fireflies, they were able to see ahead.

The three couples had been trudging in silence for
some time, keeping a sharp lookout for any kind of
strange figure.

"Guess the ghost is gone," Nancy thought.

Suddenly Bess grabbed Dave's arm. With her other
hand she pointed to a strange glob of greenish light
which grew brighter and brighter.

The six young people were astounded. A short distance ahead of them was one of the queerest-looking
figures they had ever seen. Was he a man or a beast? He
had a man-like body, but a shaggy coat of fur completely covered the creature. The head and body were
iridescent.

"Shall we attack it?" Ned whispered to Nancy.

Her answer was, "Let's separate and surround the
spook."

Before they could move, the strange creature intoned
in a deep voice, "Leave these woods at once!"

"Why should we?" George called out defiantly.

The reply made Bess quiver. "If you do not go,
trouble awaits you!"

"What do you say, Nancy?" Ned asked in a low
voice.

The young sleuth still felt they should try to capture
the ghost. Word was sent from one to another. They
spread out in a circle, then began to close in.

Suddenly the green light went out and the iridescent

figure disappeared. The searchers moved forward to the spot where he had stood. He was not there.

"He must be supernatural!" Bess said shakily.

Burt declared the earth must have swallowed him.

"I think," Dave declared, "that the guy was wearing a special suit. He quickly took it off, turned it inside out, and ran off before we completed our circle."

Nancy agreed this was the most reasonable explanation. She turned on her flashlight and began hunting for footprints. Large, animal-like prints were visible.

"Let's follow them!" she suggested.

They led through tangled undergrowth and became undetectable. Nancy followed the direction in which they had pointed. Her friends were close behind.

In a few minutes she saw a log lying across a little stream. She went over this natural bridge and found footprints on the other side. Ned was directly behind her but the others had not followed.

"Come on!" she called. "Here are more footprints—or I should say a man's shoe prints."

George came over the log next, then Burt, then Bess. Just as she reached the group, they heard a loud grunt at their rear.

They turned quickly. Dave Evans was not with them. Bess called out in alarm, "Dave! Where are you?"

There was no reply. At once the others rushed back across the log. When they reached the other side, Bess beamed her flashlight around.

"Dave!" she screamed.

Her date lay sprawled on the ground, face down. He did not move.

Quickly Burt and Ned knelt beside him. Then Ned

announced, "He's breathing, but he was knocked out pretty hard."

"How frightful!" Bess murmured.

Nancy asked herself, "Was the blow from the fall? Or was it a hand-delivered knockout, perhaps by the ghostly figure?"

·14·

Overboard!

A DISCUSSION followed among Nancy's friends whether they should let Dave lie still for a little while or carry him down to the cabin. The vote was for helping him down to the cabin.

"And let's start," Bess urged.

Dave was gently turned on his back. Nancy kept track of his pulse, while Bess took a scented handkerchief from her pocket and held it under his nostrils.

A few minutes later Dave opened his eyes and glanced around. He closed them again, but said, "Something hit me on the back of the head. I have a terrible headache."

"Better stay where you are," George advised.

She went towards the tiny mountain stream and dampened her handkerchief. Upon returning she laid it on Dave's forehead.

"That feels good," he said. Breathing deeply, he added, "And something smells mighty refreshing."

Dave looked up once more. This time he tried to get up but faltered.

"Take it easy there!" Burt said, putting a hand under one shoulder.

Dave was still a little groggy. He shook his head a few

times and took several deep breaths.

"I'll be okay," he assured the others.

"But no more sleuthing tonight," Bess insisted. "Not for any of us. It's just too dangerous in these woods—especially after dark."

The others agreed but said they would come back in the daylight and continue working on the mystery.

"I'd like to find the guy who socked me," Dave said.

"And I'd like to take care of him for you," Ned offered, his eyes flashing.

It was a slow trek down the mountainside but finally they reached the cabin and Dave went to bed at once. Aunt Eloise and Matt were very solicitous, and after checking Dave, concluded that he would not need a doctor.

No one else felt sleepy. They all gathered in the living room to talk in subdued tones. The conversation returned to the mystery of the child's sunken coach.

"Nancy, let's see that valentine you told us about," Ned requested.

She went for it and laid the memento carefully on the table. Matt and the boys admired the quaint cover with the name Maud Jayson so cleverly worked into the scroll design.

Then Nancy opened it and read the poem aloud:

" 'Ever faithful to thee
And the memory of the little lass
Her lovely pony coach
Lying 'neath the Glimmerglass
NOE
    5   R' ' "

Nancy explained who R was, then asked, "Any theories about that code?"

When no one answered, she went on, "I'm sure that the poet must have been referring to Otsego Lake and perhaps to this mirror-clear bay."

"I'll bet you're right!" George exclaimed.

After studying the valentine, Ned suggested that the N and the E might well mean northeast.

Nancy nodded as Burt asked, "But what is that five under the backward letter C?"

She thought over the question a few moments, then replied, "It could stand for Five Mile Point across the lake."

Nancy explained that the jut of land was about five miles' distance from Cooperstown.

Aunt Eloise spoke up. "They tell a story about the Point. The man who owned it at one time went off on a long trip. While he was away, the people of Cooperstown used it for a picnic and swimming area.

"When he returned, they all hoped that he would make it a public park. Instead he chased everyone off the grounds and threatened anyone who trespassed with arrest."

"The old meany!" George burst out.

Bess asked what was located northeast from Five Mile Point. She speculated that the code might refer to some spot beyond the bay.

Nancy produced a map of the area and drew a straight line from Five Mile Point directly northeast. She ended the line on the opposite side of the bay from Aunt Eloise's cottage.

"That's directly to the east of Glimmerglass Park," Burt pointed out.

"Let's go there early tomorrow morning," George proposed.

Everyone agreed and Nancy suggested they take tools with them—picks, rakes, and a crowbar. By morning Dave was feeling like himself again and insisted upon going.

Ned said he would like to try out the *Crestwood* and asked Nancy to sail to the search site with him. "We'll go across the lake first, then back to the bay."

She smiled. "That would be fun but we'll have to anchor a ways offshore. The water's rather shallow there for some distance out."

The other young people would go in Ned's open sports car. Aunt Eloise had some errands in the village and Matt offered to accompany her.

He grinned. "We may even take a long ride so Eloise can show me the sights."

Nancy, George, and Bess were very much pleased about this new friendship.

"If we're not back by lunchtime," Nancy said, "we'll picnic at Glimmerglass Park. By the way, will you stop at Miss Armitage's and give her the valentine? I think it will be safer there."

"I'll be glad to," her aunt replied.

All the young people put on swimsuits and carried the scuba gear. The two couples went off in the car. Nancy and Ned hurried down to the dock and climbed aboard the *Crestwood*.

Ned ran up the nylon sail and Nancy took the tiller. It was a beautiful morning, but the water was so calm there was barely enough breeze to gain headway. By tacking Ned managed to move slowly into the middle of the lake.

Only a few boats were out. One of them, a speedboat, was roaring towards them from the direction of Cooperstown. The pilot seemed to be making a beeline for the *Crestwood*. Didn't he see their sailboat? Or was he deliberately trying to harm the couple?

Ned and Nancy manoeuvred towards the west side of the lake. The oncoming speedboat veered in their direction.

"He's crazy!" Ned exclaimed. "Get ready to dive, Nancy."

Just as the motor-boat neared them the pilot, who was alone, turned the wheel sharply, causing great waves that rocked the sailboat violently. He steered on, but within seconds swerved back. This time he passed the *Crestwood* on the other side at such speed that towering swells formed.

Nancy and Ned were working furiously to keep their craft from capsizing. Nancy got a quick look at the name of their tormentor's boat.

The Water Witch!

She had no time to speculate about the man's indentity. Was he an accomplice of the girl who had tried to run over Bess in the same craft?

"That guy's a fiend!" Ned cried out.

The pilot made another sweeping circle around the *Crestwood*. This time the waves were too powerful for the sailboat to withstand. It capsized, throwing Nancy and Ned into the water. Instantly the motor-boat took off, roaring back towards Cooperstown.

After their plunge, the couple clung to their overturned craft.

"He's wicked!" Nancy cried angrily.

In a few moments she and Ned began trying to right

the *Crestwood*. Though the sail was made of a light nylon fabric, it was heavy enough to hamper their efforts.

Nancy swam around to the fallen mast and strained to lift the sail while Ned tugged at the other side of the boat. It was no use.

"I'll have to haul in the sheet," he said.

Fortunately their friends, already in the water, had seen the accident in the distance. They had also noticed someone coming into the bay from the head of the lake. Yo was piloting his little outboard.

"We need a ride!" George shouted at him as he approached.

"Two of you climb aboard," he said. Then he noticed the overturned craft. "Who's that out in the lake?"

When he heard the names Nancy and Ned, he revved to full speed the instant George and Burt were in his boat. Within minutes the *Crestwood* was righted and the sheet hoisted. "It will dry quickly," Nancy thought. Water which still remained in the sailboat was bailed out.

Yo asked, "What made you go over?"

Nancy told him and added, "By the way, did you find out who owns the *Water Witch*?"

"Yes. But they've rented it to a couple, Mr and Mrs Welch. Sorry but I forgot the man's first name."

"Was it Samuel or Michael, by any chance?" Nancy asked.

Yo's face lit up. "How'd you know that? It was Michael."

Nancy was delighted with the information. Now she had a very good lead to the enemies who were harassing her and her friends.

"I'll make further inquiries at that dock next time we go the Cooperstown," she determined.

Nancy and Ned sailed to the area where they wanted to search, while Yo took Burt and George back there. He waved goodbye and chugged off.

There were many sunbathers on the public beach of Glimmerglass Park, and picnickers at tables. Nancy thought her group was far enough away not to be noticed, but she was wrong. Within a short time they were besieged by the questions of curious onlookers, some on foot, others in small boats.

One precocious boy in a canoe called out with a smirk, "What you hunting for? A sunken treasure?"

·15·

Burglars!

DESPITE the annoying onlookers, and their attempts at humour, Nancy and her friends went on with the search for the child's royal coach. The boys worked with the tools they had brought, until the water was murky and they could no longer see what they were doing.

The divers gathered on the surface and swam to shallow water. Here they held a conference and all came to the conclusion that anything buried deep could be located only with a probe. Unfortunately they had forgotten to include the underwater metal detector.

"We must remember to bring it along the next time we come to hunt for the coach," Nancy remarked.

"Anybody hungry but me?" Bess called out.

George answered, "Yes. Let's go back. Say, who wants to join a swimming race to our cottage?"

"Count me out," Bess said. "I've had enough excercise."

"Me, too," added Dave and slipped his arm around her shoulders.

They offered to drive the car back. Nancy and Ned had to sail the *Crestwood* to their dock.

Burt grinned and accepted George's challenge. In order for Nancy and Ned to race them, they kept the

Crestwood alongside the swimmers. First George pulled ahead, then Burt.

"George is a wonder in the water," Ned said admiringly. "She could race on a man's swim team any time."

Nancy smiled. "Who do you think is going to win?" she asked. "I'm betting on George."

Ned heaved a sigh. "I can't go back on my own sex so I'll say Burt."

His date was still smiling. "But you're not too convinced."

As they neared shore, the racers were pulling together in perfect rhythm. Their fingers touched the dock at the same instant. The two swimmers laughed. They climbed out of the water and went to the cottage.

Ned turned to Nancy as he took down the sheet and secured the *Crestwood*. "We both win and we both lose our bet." In mock congratulations the couple shook hands.

Bess and Dave had been there for several minutes and had started luncheon preparations.

"Um! Something smells great!" Burt remarked, smacking his lips.

Bess replied slyly, "We're having snail soup and broiled grasshoppers. Do you like them?"

Burt made a wry face as Bess knew he would, then she said, "Today's menu is cream of tomato soup, ham-and-cheese sandwiches, and water-melon. Okay?"

"Okay plus," Burt replied.

"For me, too," added George.

As soon as Nancy and Ned were dressed, they came out to the porch where Aunt Eloise and Matt were talking. Miss Drew said she had a surprise for them.

"A man from the yacht club stopped here soon after you had gone," she explained. "He extended a personal invitation to you both to enter one of the sailboat races this afternoon."

"How thrilling!" Nancy exclaimed.

"He said it would not be necessary for you to let him know," Aunt Eloise went on, "but if you can participate, be at the club dock by two-thirty. The race starts at three o'clock."

"That's great!" Nancy cried. "Want to do it, Ned?"

"I sure do. But first I think we'd better slick up the *Crestwood* a bit. After her bath, she looks a little the worse for wear."

He and Nancy went down to examine the sailboat.

"If there's any quick-drying paint around this place, I can give the *Crestwood* a coat," he offered.

Everyone scrounged around the cabin and finally found an unopened can of quick-drying white paint. The sailboat was propped up on the shore. While Nancy wiped off spots from the sail, Ned rapidly sprayed on the shiny liquid. In a short time the *Crestwood* looked like new. Meanwhile, George and Burt had been washing out the inside. Soon that too was spick-and-span.

"She looks great!" Bess called from the porch. "Lunch is ready! Come and get it!"

They all were very hungry and ate every bit of the meal Bess had prepared. Then Nancy and Ned went to change into white shirts and shorts.

"Good luck!" Matt said as they left the porch. "We'll drive around to the other side of the lake and watch the race."

The group went down to the dock and the *Crestwood* was put in the water. As Nancy and Ned were about to set off, Aunt Eloise said, "Wait a minute! I forgot to give you the paper the man left which will identify you as entrants in the race."

"I'll get it," Bess offered. "Where is the paper?"

Miss Drew said the envelope was on the bureau in her room, next to her bag.

Nancy spoke up. "I really ought to have my sunglasses with me. Bess, would you mind bringing them also? They're in my handbag."

Bess hurried towards the cabin, and disappeared inside. She was gone several minutes and the others wondered why she was taking so long.

Aunt Eloise remarked, "The paper was easy to find."

She had barely said this when Bess appeared at the doorway. She cried out at the top of her voice, "Come quickly! We've been robbed!"

Everyone was stunned. Nancy and Ned leaped off the *Crestwood* and followed the others, who were already rushing across the dock and up to the porch.

"Your bag is gone, Aunt Eloise!" Bess told her. "Nancy's too!"

"What!" the group chorused.

George made a beeline for her room. At first glance nothing looked disturbed. But when she yanked open the dressing-table drawer she saw that both Bess's handbag and her own were missing.

"This is terrible!" George thought angrily.

Upon closer examination, she reported that the fleet burglar or burglars had rifled various letters and other papers in the drawer.

Just then Dave came from the boys' bedroom.

"Somebody's been through Matt's suitcase!" he exclaimed.

Everyone agreed that the intruder must have been hunting for something other than money. What could it have been?

"One thing is certain," Matt remarked. "The thief or thieves have been casing this place. Otherwise they never could have done such a complete job so quickly."

Dave hurried up the path to the road and looked up and down but there was no one in sight and no car except the ones that belonged to Nancy and to Ned.

"At least they weren't stolen," Dave said to himself.

Finally everyone gathered in the living room. Nancy glanced at her wrist watch. Goodness!" she exclaimed. "Ned, if we don't leave at once, we'll miss the race!"

The two dashed out to the porch, then stood in stupefied amazement. *Their sailboat was gone!*

By this time the others had followed them outside. But instead of waving them to victory, they too stared unbelievingly.

George was the first to speak. She cried out, "What a horrible trick! I'll bet the same person or persons who robbed our cabin took that sailboat!"

Her friends agreed. Nancy had been very quiet. Not only was she disappointed, but extremely worried. Her Aunt Eloise had important personal items in her handbag which she did not want to lose. Credit and charge account cards could easily be used by some stranger and her driver's licence also.

Nancy was alarmed about the loss of her own driver's licence. The thief might have been the girl who resembled her and would use her licence.

Matt offered to drive into town and report the loss to the police. He said nothing was missing from his suitcase. After the group had made a list of stolen articles, Matt went off with it.

Nancy was thinking, "Oh, if Yo would only come along now, he might help us. But I suppose he's down watching the races."

As if in answer to her wish, however, within ten minutes Yo pulled up to the dock of Mirror Bay Bide-A-Wee.

"I came to see what happened to you," he said. "I heard you were going to be in the race but you didn't come."

Quickly the situation was explained to him.

"Stolen!" he cried out. "Well, we'll just overtake that thief! Climb in here!"

Nancy and Ned got aboard and the search began. They had no idea which way to go.

"Yo," said Nancy, "if you were trying to hide a sailboat on this lake what spot would you pick?"

He answered instantly. "Where Shadow Brook empties into the lake."

"Then let's go there," she suggested.

Yo proved to be right. When they reached the brook, there was the half-sunken *Crestwood*. But the sleek craft did not look as it had when Nancy and Ned were ready to set sail. The sheet was torn and the craft was covered with mud.

"Some people's idea of a joke is pretty foul," Yo spoke up. "I don't know whether we can get this afloat or not."

"We can try," Nancy said.

The three of them waded into the muddy water. In

moments it had turned their white attire brown. With Yo's assistance they tugged and yanked first on one end of the sailboat, then the other.

The trio finally righted the *Crestwood,* but it could not float with the heavy mud and debris in it. Using their hands as shovels they finally cleared away most of the muck.

"I'll tow you," Yo said.

The rope was attached to the back of the motor-boat. Then Nancy climbed in beside Yo, and Ned sat in the rear of the craft to keep the sailboat from bumping into the outboard motor.

The group finally reached the Bide-A-Wee dock. Their friends had been watching for them and now rushed down to hear the story.

Everyone thanked Yo so profusely he became very much embarrassed. He said over and over again, "Oh that's all right. I'm just sorry you all missed the race."

He went off and Nancy and Ned changed into swim-suits for a dip in the bay. While the couple was in the water they saw Miss Armitage arrive and go inside the cottage. For this reason Nancy and Ned took only a short swim. Then they pulled themselves up on to the dock and wrapped big towels around them. The next moment the caller stepped on to the porch with Bess and they waved to her.

Bess called down excitedly, "Nancy and Ned, come up here quick! Wait until you hear what happened to Miss Armitage!"

· 16 ·

A Valuable Witness

"It happened today," Bess announced.

Nancy and Ned listened carefully as Miss Armitage began to speak excitedly.

"It was dreadful—dreadful! I had been on a shopping trip and arrived home, with my arms full of groceries. I quietly put the key into the door and opened it. Suddenly I became aware of a slight sound in my bedroom."

The woman closed her eyes as if the recollection were painful. Nancy asked quietly, "Did you investigate?"

Miss Armitage nodded. "The result was both good and bad. I found a man rummaging through my desk drawer. He was the ugliest human being I've ever seen. I couldn't even describe his face. It was grotesque. He looked like an animal."

"Probably," Nancy suggested, "he was wearing a rubber mask."

"Perhaps," the woman conceded. "Anyway, I was horrified to see that in one hand he had the precious valentine! In the other he held the pieces of the torn letter telling about the child's royal coach."

"Then what happened?" Ned prompted her, as she paused.

"The man turned and looked at me. I said, 'Put those down and get out of here!' All he did was glare at me for a few seconds. I had a sudden inspiration and threw all my packages at him hard."

"Good for you!" George burst out.

"He was taken off guard," the woman went on, "and I was able to grab the valentine and slip it under my pillow when he wasn't looking. Then I tried to get the letter. By this time he had recovered his wits. He knocked me down so hard I fainted."

"How dreadful!" Nancy said. "While you were unconscious, did he take anything else?"

Miss Armitage shook her head. "Fortunately no. I had only a little money with me. It was in a pocket. More money and credit cards were safely locked up. I have a feeling that the man was not a regular burglar; rather, that he had come to steal only the valentine and letter."

"Then in some way he's connected with the secret of Mirror Bay," Nancy remarked. "I wonder if he's the person who burglarized our cabin."

This possibility was discussed pro and con. Aunt Eloise told Miss Armitage they suspected the girl who resembled Nancy of being part of a gang.

"We feel that she's working with two of them who live or work up on the mountain."

Ned asked Miss Armitage if she had called the police.

"Oh yes. They came at once. I didn't want to tell them about the valentine and the stolen letter because I'm trying to keep that a secret—I just told them about the man in my house. They didn't know of anyone around here who has a grotesque face such as I described and suggested, as you did, Nancy, that he may have been wearing a mask."

Aunt Eloise asked Miss Armitage if she would have dinner with them, but she declined.

"I'm expecting some friends this evening." She smiled ruefully. "I'll really have something interesting to tell them!"

The caller stood up, and after warning everyone to be extremely careful, said goodbye.

When she had gone, Nancy said, "I'm afraid that though Miss Armitage is trying to keep her mystery a secret, one or more persons besides us know about it."

"And I'm afraid you're right," Aunt Eloise added.

They had an early dinner. Then Dave announced that he wanted to put the sailboat in tip-top shape.

"I haven't been much help since someone in the woods knocked me out," he said. "Now it's my turn."

Bess joined him. Just as they reached the dock, Yo arrived in his little motor-boat.

"Hi, everybody!" he shouted loudly.

Nancy had a hunch the young man was bringing a message to her and hurried down the porch steps and along the dock.

"I have news for you," he said. "I found out more about the *Water Witch* that was rented to Mr and Mrs Michael Welch. They've turned it in."

"What!" Nancy exclaimed. "Nothing else?"

The young detective was disappointed at Yo's negative reply. She had hoped to find out if Mrs Welch was the girl who resembled her and if her husband was the mysterious green man in the woods.

Aloud she said, "Thanks a lot for the information, Yo." She grinned at him. "You're really getting to be a detective. Well, keep up the good work. All clues are acceptable to Nancy Drew and company."

Yo laughed. By this time Ned had joined Nancy on the dock. The Cooperstown boy looked at him and said, "Did you ever hear about the girl hitch-hiker who turned out to be a ghost?"

"Let's hear about her," Ned urged.

Nancy thought she detected a twinkle in his eyes. She had a hunch Ned knew the story but wanted to hear Yo's version of it.

"Well," Yo began, "this happened outside a town not too far from here. It was over a hundred years ago."

Nancy spoke up. "Which means nobody can prove or disprove it now."

Yo insisted the story was true. "A young man was driving along in a buggy. It had started to rain hard and he'd dropped the front curtain. As he passed a cemetery, he saw a girl dressed all in white standing at the roadside. She waved at him to stop. Of course he did and opened the curtain wide enough for her to get into the buggy."

Yo said that she gave him an address in town and asked to be taken there. He wondered why she was dressed in such a filmy, evening-type dress. Then he thought perhaps she had been walking home alone from a party.

"She did not say another word and he asked no questions. When they reached the address, he stopped the horse, got out of the buggy, and helped her up the front steps of the house. He rang the bell, then turned around to see if his horse was all right.

"As the woman opened the door he turned back to watch the girl go inside. To his surprise she was not there. She had vanished completely!"

"What a strange tale!" Nancy remarked.

Ned was trying hard to keep from grinning. "Yes, it is," he agreed. "The fellow with the buggy was so amazed he could hardly speak.

"But finally he said to the woman, 'At the cemetery I picked up a girl who wanted to come here but she suddenly disappeared!'

"He felt very foolish of course, but the woman smiled tolerantly and said, 'This happens every rainy night. That was the ghost of my daughter. She was buried in that cemetery four years ago.'"

Yo's eyes grew large. "Say, you beat all! I thought sure I had you stumped this time. Where'd you learn the rest of that story?"

Ned mentioned his study of folklore in a psychology course.

"As a matter of fact, it is one of my favourites. For your information, Yo, that particular ghost story has appeared in one form or another in almost every country of the world."

Yo scratched his thick hair. "I got to be going now, but I'll have some more spooky stories for you next time we meet."

Nancy and Ned waved goodbye to the young man, then paused to see how Bess and Dave were progressing. Cleaning the mud from the sailboat was not an easy task but the industrious couple said they would keep on until dark.

When Nancy and Ned came up to the cabin porch, Burt met them. "The baseball museum in Cooperstown," he said, "is open until nine o'clock tonight. Let's go there and look around."

Bess and Dave decided to finish their work and Aunt Eloise had seen the exhibition the previous summer.

Matt accompanied Burt and the other young people in Nancy's convertible. When they reached town, Ned, who was driving, parked the car along Main Street. The group crossed to the other side and entered the Baseball Hall of Fame.

After they had looked at various plaques and busts of outstanding players Nancy remarked, "I didn't realize until now that there were this many famous men in one sport!"

They paused at the showcase containing Babe Ruth's uniform and Ned remarked, "I think he was the greatest of all time."

"Why?" Matt asked.

"Because," Ned replied, "he was equally good as a pitcher and a batter."

The five sightseers walked along in silence for a while, reading the plaques and looking at the favourite bats of well-known hitters and famous balls that had won games.

Matt told the others that the player he most admired was Lou Gehrig. "What a record!" he said. "He played 2,130 consecutive games in fourteen seasons with the New York Yankees. His lifetime batting average was ·341."

"I believe he batted in 150 or more runs in seven different seasons," Ned added.

Nancy smiled. "You'd never guess who I'm partial to. It's not because of his record but something he said. A quotation from Leroy Satchel Paige.

" *'Don't look back—something might be gaining on you.'* "

The others agreed this was great advice, not only in a baseball game, but also in life.

Matt nodded. "Too many people waste time trying

to see who's behind them instead of advancing to the next base."

When they finished their tour, it was nearly time for the museum to close. Matt and the young people left. As they were about to cross the street to her car, Nancy noticed a bus at the kerb. The driver stood under a bright street light.

"Look!" she exclaimed. "There's the man who drove the bus Aunt Eloise arrived in. Maybe that girl swindler has been on his route. I want to talk to him!"

She raced up the street.

·17·

The Girl Captive

BEFORE Nancy could reach the bus driver, he hopped aboard his vehicle and took off. She ran even faster, hoping to catch up to him. Fortunately he had to stop at a red traffic light.

He looked very much surprised to see Nancy. Hesitantly he opened the door and let her climb aboard. "I'm not going to New York on this trip," he said. "Just to another town to pick up some folks at a conference."

As the light changed and the bus pulled ahead, he said to Nancy, "So the police haven't caught up with you yet! You know—" he paused—"I ought to turn you in myself!"

For a moment Nancy was taken aback, then realized he thought she was the girl who resembled her.

She said quickly, "I'm not the person you think I am. But evidently you know the girl who looks like me and is wanted by the police. A lot of other people are trying to find her, including me. She's guilty of several things besides cheating those poor men and women who were stranded after the bus trip."

The driver turned his head slightly to take a look at Nancy.

"I see now you're a different girl. What else has the other one done?"

Nancy told him about the *Water Witch* episode on the lake when the boat had almost hit Bess; of the suspicion that the girl had been involved in the theft at the cottage; and the burglary at the jewellery store.

Noticing his name on an identification card above the dashboard, Nancy asked, "Mr Patterson, did the girl ever mention her name to you?"

The bus driver said, "Yes. It's Doria Sampler. At least that's what she told me on the first trip she made up here. She came up several times, but I haven't seen her in a long while."

Nancy inquired if he could give her any other information which would be helpful in locating Doria.

"Not much," Patterson replied. "She did say Sampler was her maiden name, but I noticed she was wearing a wedding ring. I asked her about it, and she admitted having a husband. Let's see. She mentioned his name but I can't recall what it was."

Nancy asked him if the name Michael Welch sounded familiar. The driver shook his head. Next she inquired if it might have been Sam something.

"That's it!" the driver replied. "Sam Hornsby."

Nancy smiled broadly. "You've been wonderful. I suppose Doria didn't tell you anything about her husband?"

Patterson laughed. "I guess that young woman is a great kidder. She said he was a green man. I asked her what she meant by that, but she just giggled and said, 'Did you ever hear of male witches?' "

The driver was sure the girl was joking and said she seemed to be nice enough. When he had heard from the charter bus drivers about her cheating a lot of people, he was amazed.

"It's hard to believe," he muttered to himself.

Nancy asked, "Do you know where this Sam Hornsby is now?"

"No, I don't."

The driver said he had no more information. Nancy was delighted with what she had learned and thanked him.

"I'll get off now," she told him.

By this time they were some distance out of town. He asked in concern, "How are you going to get back to the village?"

Nancy had noticed that Ned and the others were following in her car.

"I see that my friends are right behind the bus," she answered, "so I'll get off at the next crossroad."

Mr Patterson wished Nancy luck in her detective work. "I hope you track down this Doria Sampler Hornsby."

Then he opened the door. Nancy said goodbye and jumped off. She waved to him as he pulled away.

As she stepped into the car, Ned smiled at her and said, "I can tell from your eyes that you had some luck talking to that driver. What did you learn?"

Nancy told her surprising news and concluded by saying, "I'd like to go up on the mountain and hunt for the green man."

George chanted:

> "Sam, Sam, the green man,
> Avoid Nancy Drew if you can!"

The others laughed. Burt added, "And that goes for Doria too."

Ned turned the car around and they headed back to Cooperstown. Presently Matt looked at his watch. He informed the others that it was ten o'clock.

"Do you think there'll be any activity up in the woods at this hour?" he asked.

Nancy shrugged. "Things happened pretty late the other times we were up there."

She wondered if Matt were tired and this was a diplomatic way of coaxing them all home instead of climbing the mountain. By now they had rounded the curve into East Lake Road. Suddenly their headlights picked up the figure of a young woman on foot scooting up the hillside.

"That's Doria!" Nancy exclaimed. "Now's our chance to capture her!"

As soon as the car stopped they jumped out. Ned locked it, and the five pursuers started after the girl.

"This is a long way from where we saw the green man," George remarked.

Nancy surmised that Doria was taking a direct line to the place where her husband was hiding.

"Could it be the lean-to where I found the bobbie pins?" Nancy asked herself. "But she's heading towards Natty Bumppo's cave. Maybe she's going to hide in there. I guess she knows that our headlights picked her up and she can hear us following her."

They reached the cave made famous by James Fenimore Cooper in his *Leatherstocking Tales*. Their flashlights revealed no one inside. They hurried on through the woods. Here and there the searchers could see a fresh shoe print and kept on climbing.

"She's fast," Burt remarked. "We'd better double our speed or we'll never catch her."

There was no more conversation as Nancy and her friends dashed among the trees towards the summit. Nancy took the lead, beaming her flashlight in a great circle.

"I see her! I see her! We've caught up!" she cried excitedly.

The pursuers ran even faster and within another half minute they had surrounded Doria Sampler Hornsby.

"What's the meaning of this?" she asked defiantly. "Get lost! All of you!"

Nancy and her friends closed in on the girl. When she tried to break away, Matt put a strong hand on her shoulder. But she wiggled loose.

"Don't you dare touch me!" she screamed. "Go away! Leave me alone!"

Suddenly the captured girl began to fight like a tiger. She used her fingernails as claws and slashed at one, then another of her captors.

"Hey!" Burt cried in pain as her nails dug into his arm.

Doria's eyes blazed and her face grew red. When anyone came near her, she kicked at him.

"All this won't do you any good," said Nancy as Ned wrenched the girl from Burt. "I'm tired of having people accuse *me* of being a lawbreaker. We're taking you to the sheriff!"

"You'll do nothing of the sort!" Doria cried out. "I can't help it if I look like you, Nancy Drew. But that doesn't make me the guilty person. You can't prove a thing against me."

Before Nancy had a chance to answer, George spoke up. "Oh no? How about all those phony hotel reservations you sold to people for a vacation at Cooperstown?"

Doria insisted that she had not sold the tickets. She was ignorant of the whole swindle and was just as amazed as the passengers when she learned about it.

"Then who did sell the tickets?" Nancy asked. "We understood you were acting as agent."

"I won't say another word," Doria replied.

Nancy reminded her that she had used the *Water Witch* to deliberately run down one of her friends.

Doria answered quickly, "I didn't see her. She was underwater."

"Is your husband Sam Hornsby mixed up in the racket?" Ned inquired.

Doria suddenly looked wild-eyed. Instead of making a break for liberty or fighting her captors any more, she sat down on the ground and buried her face in her hands. She began to weep.

The onlookers stared at one another. Were her tears genuine or was Doria putting on an act to gain their sympathy so that they would not turn her over to the police?

Matt answered their questioning thoughts. "Don't be misled," he advised.

Nancy had not finished interrogating the girl. Now she went and sat alongside her.

"I'm sorry everything is such a mess," she said. "Doria, maybe you are innocent. Is your husband the green man? I mean, does he use the disguise to scare people away? Tell me why. Things will go easier for you."

Doria did not answer nor did she raise her eyes.

There was silence for half a minute, then Matt spoke up. "I think I know the reason why Hornsby puts on those spook acts."

All eyes turned to Matt. Everyone waited expectantly for him to explain.

·18·

A Cage of Light

"ONE day," Matt began, "I attended a private dinner for scientists on the subject of cold light. One of the men, Martin Larramore, told us the high points of a discovery of his. He had nearly perfected a formula, using the phenomenon of fireflies, and expected to complete it soon. A short time after the speech all his blueprints and notes were stolen."

His listeners gasped but said nothing. He continued, "Some careful detective work revealed that two renegade scientists were the probable culprits."

"What were their names?" Nancy asked.

"Michael W. Brink and Samuel H. Jones."

Matt went on to say that the two men had vanished. It was assumed they had gone to some secret place to put the finishing touches on the formula and then present it as their own.

"I have a strong feeling that the pair may be in these very woods." He turned to Doria. "Are they?"

There was no reply. Although the suspect had made no comment during Matt's astounding revelation, she had listened intently. Her eyes were like burning coals and full of hatred for her captors.

The professor continued. He said Larramore had

mentioned that the unknown quantity in the formula directly involved fireflies.

George spoke up. "So this would be an ideal time and place for those renegade scientists to work. There are lots of fireflies here and certainly it is a secluded spot."

Nancy agreed. "Do you know what I suspect? That Welch and Hornsby may be Michael's and Sam's middle names."

At this Doria jumped but still she said nothing. It was only a moment later that George noticed the young woman trying to inch away from the group.

"She may try to escape!" George thought, and moved nearer her.

Doria looked at the girl in dismay. She could not flee from her captors!

As Matt finished his story about the renegade scientists, he turned to Doria. "I'm giving you a choice of leading us to these men or of being taken directly to the sheriff."

His remark was followed by a prolonged period of silence as the others watched Doria closely. Her expression did not change.

"Okay!" Matt said. "Let's go!"

Once more the captured girl pleaded innocence but no one paid any attention to her. She was prodded along and carefully guarded.

As they reached the foot of the mountainside, and headed for Nancy's convertible, a State Police car came along. Ned hailed it and the driver stopped.

"What's going on here?" asked the officer beside him.

He turned a flashlight directly into the faces of the group. Doria instantly covered hers with one hand.

"Is something wrong, miss?" the other officer asked her.

Nancy introduced herself and quickly explained, "This young woman is the one wanted in connection with that vacation hoax."

"Congratulations," the driver remarked. "We've been looking everywhere for her."

"We think she's been hiding up in the woods," Nancy replied.

The officer said it would not be necessary for Nancy or any of the others to come with them, since they had a warrant for the young woman's arrest. "What is your name?" he asked the prisoner.

She still refused to answer, so Nancy replied, "Doria Sampler Hornsby."

She purposely did not mention Matt's suspicion about the two renegade scientists up in the woods. Actually the young sleuth and her friends had no concrete evidence against them.

As soon as the police had driven away with their prisoner, Nancy announced that she would like to climb right back up the mountainside and try to find Welch and Hornsby. The others were eager to go, so all of them set off once more.

They followed the path to the point where they had captured Doria, then looked for shoe prints and trodden grass. They were able to detect an indistinct trail.

"I think that we should be as quiet as possible," Ned warned. "We don't want to scare the men away if they're in the area."

George grinned. "Nor give Sam a chance to put on one of his scare costumes."

The five trudged along in silence, with Nancy, Ned,

and Matt in the lead. Finally they reached the spot where Nancy had overheard the conversation between Sam and Mike.

There were voices again!

One man was saying, "I'm worried. Doria should've been back by this time. Something must have happened to her."

Another voice said, "You worry too much. First it's Doria, then the police and then those people in the cabin. Try to calm down."

"That's all right for you to say," retorted the man whose voice Nancy now recognized as Sam's. "But she happens to be my wife. I'm going to look for her."

"Have it your own way," Michael answered. "But what makes you think you'll find her? Remember, she said something about taking a trip to New York City."

Sam did not answer. Instead he said, "Listen, Mike, if anyone starts snooping round, put on my green suit or the ghost outfit."

The excited listeners realized now that the voices were coming from underground! Nancy waved her friends back, indicating they were to station themselves behind trees. She herself chose one nearby, so she could watch carefully.

Half a minute later she saw a tangled mass of briers rise up from the earth. A camouflaged wooden trap-door! A man climbed from the pit.

He was about to close the trap-door when his partner called up, "I'm coming with you. It's too dangerous for you to go alone."

Both men had flashlights and by their beams the hidden group could see the strangers' faces plainly.

Nancy and George had never seen either of them before.

As they walked away, Nancy noted that the one she associated with Sam's voice walked with a slightly uneven gait. His shoe prints undoubtedly matched those the girls had found a few days earlier. Michael was taller and walked with a straight stride.

As soon as the suspects were out of sight and hearing, the group gathered. Nancy suggested, "Let's investigate that pit while we have the chance."

Ned and Matt were game but thought someone should keep a lookout. George and Burt offered.

"If somebody is coming, I'll give our special bird call," George told Nancy.

The trap-door was lifted. Attached to the side of the pit was a rope ladder. Matt climbed down first, then Ned and finally Nancy. The three found themselves in an amazingly large well-lit cavern.

Undoubtedly it was man-made. Nancy wondered if during the occupation of Indians at Otsego the boys in the tribe had used it either for ceremonies or for play.

"Pioneer soldiers may even have camped here," she said to herself.

There was a centre section with a room on either side. One of these proved to be a laboratory. The other was a huge cage of fine-mesh wire filled with fireflies. Most of them were roosting in an artificial tree. The light they created together was dazzling.

Apparently the centre section of the pit was used for living purposes, since there were three beds, a stove, and a refrigerator.

"Three beds indicate that Doria may stay here," Nancy remarked. "And look!"

Under one lay the scare costumes and several flashlights with green bulbs!

"Good evidence," Ned commented.

"I guess those men have their own electric plant," Matt remarked, looking around, "although I don't see their source of power."

Ned grinned. "Maybe the continuous twinkling of the fireflies is enough illumination for their experiments."

The visitors were so fascinated by the luminescent beetles that they watched them for several minutes.

"I can't take my eyes off them," Nancy said, interrupting the silence.

"Cold light," Matt murmured. "One of these days we'll be carrying flashlights that go off and on with the same ease, power, and cold light of these little creatures."

Ned thought they should start their search for the stolen papers.

"We don't know how long those men will be gone," he reminded Nancy and Matt.

The professor laughed. "Where Doria is now would be the last place her husband and his friend would think of looking for her."

"You mean in jail?" Nancy asked.

"That's right. And Doria wouldn't dare communicate with the men to supply bail for her."

"Maybe she couldn't get it anyway, after swindling all those people," Ned remarked.

"That's a fair guess," Matt agreed.

The three stopped talking and now began to examine the underground laboratory. The stolen notes and blueprints were not in sight. Nancy said she felt reluctant about looking in the strangers' luggage.

"Maybe we won't have to," Matt said.

He, Nancy, and Ned slowly cast their eyes about the centre room. Finally they went back to the laboratory. Under a workbench Nancy saw a small chest.

"Maybe there's something in that!" she said hopefully.

·19·

Trapped!

THE chest was heavy as Nancy soon discovered. She could not drag it out alone so Ned and Matt pulled it to the middle of the room.

"You found it, Nancy," Ned remarked. "You should open it."

In a jiffy she had lifted the lid and they all stared at the contents.

"The stolen papers!" Matt exclaimed.

Inside lay a sheaf of blueprints and several large hardcover books containing typed material.

Matt quickly examined a few of them. "This is the stolen formula," he said. "And here is Dr Larramore's name."

The three searchers agreed that they should take all the papers with them. But they were too large to be put into pockets and there was no bag or small suitcase in sight.

"We'll have to take the chest," Nancy stated, "and deliver it to the police as fast as we can."

"Right," said Ned. "Matt, I guess you and I can carry this between us."

In the meantime Nancy had taken several books out of the chest and was gazing at some objects in the bottom. "What are these things?" she asked.

Matt examined them and said they were parts of equipment for manufacturing the formula. "It won't be necessary to take these. If we leave them here, the chest will be lighter."

Carefully the various gadgets were laid on the floor under the bench and the searchers got ready to leave.

Ned warned that they had better hurry. "The men might spot us walking through the woods, and make trouble."

"Don't you think it would be better for us to hide the chest nearby and bring the police to the spot?" Matt suggested.

Nancy said that if they hid the chest in the woods, rain might soak right through it and ruin the papers.

"No matter what we do, let's get out of her," Ned insisted.

"You go first," Nancy told him.

As he and Matt lifted the chest, Ned said, "I believe I can carry this on my shoulder."

He swung the chest up and started to climb the rope ladder. At that instant they heard George give the special bird call.

"The men are coming back!" Nancy whispered. "Hurry! We mustn't be caught here!"

Matt stepped behind Ned and helped him steady the chest. Nancy waited at the foot of the ladder. She was certain their combined weight might break it.

Just then the bird call again! Burt, crouched at the edge of the pit, quickly told his friends they could escape if they would hurry.

In the next second everything seemed to happen at once. Two strange men had come down a mountain trail. One knocked Burt into the pit. The other grabbed the chest.

Both men shook the ladder, causing Ned and Matt to fall off. Instantly the attackers pulled the ladder up. The camouflaged cover was slammed shut and something heavy was rolled on top of it.

"A rock," Nancy cried out. "We're trapped!"

It took only a few seconds for the young people to collect their wits.

Nancy said, "Quick! Ned, hop on to Matt's shoulders and try to get out of here."

Ned did this, but his steady pressure against the trap-door could not lift it. He climbed down.

"I wonder where George is," Nancy said.

Burt was extremely worried. "We've *got* to get out of here!" he declared.

This time he and Ned climbed on to Matt's shoulders. By pushing hard they were able to move the obstruction a little. Then suddenly it burst open. Burt raised himself out and looked around.

George was not in sight. "George!" he shouted. There was no answer.

Nancy swung up to Matt's shoulders and climbed out. She also called her chum's name. Still there was no reply. She berated herself for having urged the trip and the search. If only it had occurred to her that pals of the renegade scientists might come to the pit! Who were the men? She asked Burt to describe them.

The description of one fitted the man in woodsman's clothing who had met the girls the first time they had gone up the mountainside. The other attacker was unfamiliar.

The rope ladder was lying on the ground. Burt set it

in place. Ned and Matt climbed out.

Anxiously Nancy and her companions discussed what had happened to George. Had she been kidnapped by the men and was one or the other responsible for trying to abduct Bess and knocking out Dave?

Once more they called George's name, but as before there was no answer to their frantic summons. They searched a wide area but could not find her.

"I'm going to the police," Burt announced.

He started down the path towards Natty Bumppo's cave. The others followed. They kept flashing their lights to see if there was any sign of George. They found no shoe prints or any marks on trees, a method Nancy, Bess, and George sometimes used to indicate a trail they had taken.

"Now what are we going to do?" Burt sighed as he paused several feet from the cave entrance.

Almost at once Burt caught sight of something gleaming in a clump of grass. Without speaking, he pointed towards it. Nancy and Ned followed him to the spot. Before them lay a metal comb!

"This might belong to George," Nancy said hopefully, and stooped to pick it up. "There are a few dark strands of hair still on it."

"I'll bet she's being held in that cave," Burt interjected with mounting concern.

Ned was less convinced. "Someone else could have dropped the comb," he said.

"It's only a hunch, but—" Nancy started to say as they edged closer to the cave entrance.

"What is?" Ned whispered. For a moment she had decided to reveal no more.

"Come on, tell us," Burt begged anxiously.

By this time they were flashing lights inside the pitch-black cave.

"Why all the suspense?" Ned asked finally. "Do you think anything serious has happened to George?"

Nancy smiled faintly. "Oh, you know me and my hunches. Sometimes they're wrong."

"Your batting average is pretty high, I'd say," Ned answered. "You could be nominated for the Baseball Hall of Fame yourself."

Nancy, whose thoughts were solely on George, did not reply to his quip. Instead she said fearfully, "I hate to tell you my hunch, but it certainly looks as if those men have kidnapped George."

In a short time they reached the road and all of them exclaimed in surprise. Nancy's car was gone!

Ned said angrily, "First those guys take the chest and kidnap George, then steal your car!"

"But how could they drive it?" Matt asked. "Don't you have the keys with you, Nancy?"

She nodded but said that both George and Bess carried duplicate sets. "Perhaps George had them in a pocket."

Burt groaned. "I get the whole picture now. Those men forced her down to the car by another route and made her hand over the keys. All the more reason why we should go to the police."

The group started trudging towards the village. They had not gone far when they had to jump to the side of the road. Two State Police cars were roaring along, heading up East Lake Road.

"Maybe they've picked up a clue to Doria's accomplices!" Ned said hopefully.

The words were hardly out of his mouth when they

heard another vehicle coming at a fast speed. To their utter amazement it was Nancy's car. Driving it was George Fayne. No one else was with her.

Instantly Nancy and the boys began to shout. George applied the brakes and came to a screeching halt a few feet ahead. The others raced towards her and started to ask questions.

She cut them short and cried out, "Jump in! Quick! I know where the thieves are!"

· 20 ·

A Royal Finish

As Nancy's car raced along East Lake Road, George explained how she had escaped from the two men.

"I saw flashlights bobbing in our direction, so I gave my first bird call. When you didn't come, Burt moved to the trap-door to warn you. I gave the bird call again but those men suddenly were at the entrance.

"I knew there was nothing I could do to help—I'd only be captured. So I decided to see what happened and then go for the police."

George told of the scene at the top of the pit from her vantage point, and the others revealed what they had found inside.

"Goodness!" George exclaimed. Then she went on, "I guess the chest was kind of heavy. Anyway, those two men took turns carrying it on their shoulders. They couldn't go very fast, so I was able to keep close enough to hear what they were saying.

"They decided to head for the old Hyde Homestead. One of them knew of an empty building there and was planning to hide the chest in it. He said they would go back for it later.

"I don't know how they expected to get there—maybe by boat. I didn't wait to find out. Instead I hurried to your car, Nancy. Thank goodness I'd put my duplicate set of keys in my pocket."

George smiled a bit ruefully. "I went to the sheriff's office in Cooperstown. At first the officer on duty didn't believe my story. He said the police had heard stories about a luminescent green man and ghosts but had never encountered any of them during their own search in the woods."

George described the clever trap-door to the pit where the renegade scientists were experimenting.

"What finally convinced him, I guess, was the fact that I said Doria Sampler was evidently married to one of those men.

"The officer went to talk with her, but though she admitted she was Mrs Sam Hornsby she would say nothing more. Anyway, the officer got in touch with the State Police, who decided to investigate empty buildings at the Hyde Homestead."

"Where's that?" Ned inquired.

Nancy explained that it was above the lake past Glimmerglass Park. "It's a beautiful mansion which stands on a high hill."

George whizzed along but had lost time picking up her passengers so the police cars were out of sight. She caught sight of them, however, when she reached the well-kept grounds of the Hyde Homestead. Two men carrying a chest were being escorted by the police to the officer's car. The young people jumped from Nancy's car and rushed towards them.

"I'm glad you got here," said one of the state troopers. "You'll be able to identify these suspects."

The prisoner, who was the woodsman the girls had met before, spoke up. "I'll admit nothing. We've done no wrong. These people here," he said, pointing towards Nancy's group, "stole this chest which belongs to friends of ours. We were only getting it back for them and hiding it in a safe place. You have no right to arrest us."

The other officer, who said his name was Brady, told the men there was plenty of evidence against them. They could do their explaining in court.

"That won't take long," Matt spoke up. "The papers and blueprints in this chest were stolen from Dr Martin Larramore."

All this time the two prisoners were glaring at Nancy and her friends. Finally one said to her, "You deserved to have trouble. The whole bunch of you were too snoopy. My pals weren't hurting anybody."

Just then a message came over the short-wave radio of the first police car. It said Samuel Hornsby Jones had been arrested. He had learned his wife was in custody and had given himself up. His buddy, Michael Welch Brink, had been apprehended a short while later.

Both men had confessed. Sam had played the parts of the green man, the ghost, and the iridescent animal-like creature.

Brink had searched Miss Armitage's cottage for the valentine and letter. The letter had been recovered from him.

Brady asked Nancy, "Do you know what this is all about?"

"All I can tell you now is that it involves a secret, but there's nothing criminal about it. Apparently Doria, Sam, and Mike were spying near our cabin and overheard us talking."

Brady informed his prisoners that the young people had captured Doria Hornsby and turned her over to the authorities.

Startled by the news, the two prisoners asked why.

Brady explained. "She is a professional thief, along with her two brothers who live in New York City. They're the ones who burglarized a jewellery store in our village and have committed other thefts. Doria said she was doing it to get money for Sam, but that neither he nor Michael knew about the vacation swindle."

Brady smiled. "Nancy Drew, your detective work apparently scared this Doria. That's why both she and the men harassed you in various ways."

"You mean like capsizing my friend Ned and me in our sailboat and burglarizing our cabin?" she asked.

When Brady nodded, Nancy inquired if all the stolen bags had been recovered.

"I'll find out," Brady offered.

He radioed headquarters again and asked. The answer was yes. The police had searched the underground cavern thoroughly. They had found not only all the handbags but a quantity of stolen jewellery.

"By the way," Brady reported, "a pal of Sam Jones tried to kidnap one of you girls and another accomplice knocked out her boy friend."

The two men whom the troopers were holding winced. They finally admitted their guilt.

Brady said that the officers would take their prisoners away. They thanked Nancy and her friends for their help and said no doubt the young sleuth would be hearing from them soon.

The State Police drove off and the others went back to Mirror Bay Bide-A-Wee.

"There's Miss Armitage's car," Nancy remarked.

As they walked up on the porch, there were sighs of relief from Miss Drew, Bess, Dave, and their caller.

"Where did you go?" Aunt Eloise asked. "You've been gone so long, we've been frantic."

Miss Armitage said she had been at the cabin for some time. "I didn't want to leave until I knew everyone was all right," she told them.

Bess and Dave, as well as the two women, gasped in astonishment upon hearing all that had happened to their friends in the past few hours.

Miss Armitage said, "I'm proud of your detective work." She smiled and her eyes twinkled. "After you've had a rest from this mystery, how about solving mine?"

Nancy promised they would go diving for the child's royal coach the following afternoon. Miss Armitage rose to leave. Dave walked to her car with her.

Everyone was too excited to retire. The mystery on the mountain was discussed over and over. Aunt Eloise and Bess served a midnight snack. Finally all of them were yawning and went to bed.

The following morning they took two cars and went to the village to church. Later, as Nancy's passengers were returning to her convertible, Bess hurried up alongside her.

"This morning I overheard Matt say to Aunt Eloise, 'After you get back to the city I'll be calling you for a date.'"

Nancy smiled. "That's great! I can't think of any nicer friend for Aunt Eloise than Matt."

About an hour after dinner, everyone changed into swimsuits. Just then Miss Armitage arrived.

"Hello, everybody!" she said. "I have a surprise for

Nancy and Ned. Are you driving over to the other side of the bay?"

"Yes," Nancy replied.

"Well, when you come up to the road, I'll show you what I have in my station wagon and transfer it to your car. In fact, that won't even be necessary because I'm going to follow you. I have a strong hunch that today you're going to find the child's Russian coach."

"We'll do our best," Nancy promised.

When she and Ned saw the surprise, they were delighted. There were two face masks with oxygen tanks. Now the couple could swim deeper and stay longer underwater!

Miss Armitage handed over the gear. When Nancy and Ned reached the search area, they adjusted the face masks and the oxygen tanks.

Nancy picked up the metal detector and Ned carried a probe. The other swimmers put on scuba diving equipment.

It was very exciting in the low depths of the bay. Fish they had never seen and plants galore grew up out of the mud floor.

As the couple swam along, Nancy listened carefully for ticks on the metal detector. After Ned had lodged the probe into the mud, he let Nancy take the lead. Suddenly she began to tread water and steadied the detector over one spot. The device was emitting a very loud, clear vibratory sound.

"This must be it!" Nancy thought. "Oh, I do hope so!"

She motioned for Ned to get the probe. He swam back for it, then placed the tool at the spot from which the sound had come. Within moments the slender instrument struck something hard. Ned kept poking the probe in and finally indicated to Nancy that they had found a large square object. The couple tried to dislodge it, but this was impossible.

They rose to the surface and swam to shore. The couple removed their masks and Nancy reported excitedly, "We think we've found the coach but we can't move it!"

Burt and Dave asked to borrow their equipment and take down some other tools.

"All right," Nancy said. "We wish you luck."

Between them the two boys managed to loosen from the mud what proved to be a large metal box. It was much too heavy for them to dredge up. They surfaced and announced that they needed strong rope or metal cable and a small derrick to lift the object on to shore.

Miss Armitage was walking up and down excitedly. The elderly woman wished she could help but said she did not have the strength.

"I wish I had proper equipment," Aunt Eloise spoke up. "I think it's going to take more than two people working down there to raise the chest."

George grinned. "How about giving Matt and me a chance at it?"

Burt and Dave removed the equipment. George and Matt put it on. They swam off into the deeper water of the bay.

In the meantime Ned remembered that he had a long coil of heavy rope in the boot of his car. "I got stuck last winter in the snow near Emerson and had to be pulled out. Ever since, I've carried the rope with me. There's also some heavy rope in that kitchen cabinet where we got the tools."

He went back to Bide-A-Wee for it. When George and Matt surfaced, he showed the rope to them.

"The chest is mighty heavy," Matt said, "but nothing ventured nothing gained. Burt, are you game to go down again?"

"Sure."

Each of them carried one end of the stout ropes, while those on shore held the other ends. They knew by the quiver of the ropes when they were being tied round the chest. Would they hold?

A few minutes later there were tugs on the lines. Ned, Dave, Nancy, Bess, and even Aunt Eloise pulled as hard as they could. They kept slipping and falling down and did not seem to be making any progress.

Beneath the water Matt and Burt simultaneously were keeping the box from being scraped against the shale while pushing it upward as hard as they could. To everyone's delight the large object finally was lugged on to the shore.

"I hope it's the right one!" Miss Armitage murmured.

Dave said to her with a grin, "This may not be a child's coach, you know. Possibly it's pirate gold!"

The remarked eased Miss Armitage's tension somewhat. She suggested that they wait to open it at Bide-A-Wee.

It was dragged up the incline and lifted into Miss Armitage's station wagon. Burt and Matt removed their masks and tanks, then quickly all the swimmers donned robes. The happy searchers climbed into the cars. Nancy and Ned said they would ride in the back of the station wagon and help steady the cumbersome box.

Finally the mysterious object was deposited on the front porch of the cabin. It was tightly sealed and everyone wondered how they could possibly prise it open.

Nancy examined the box carefully with a magnifying glass. She could barely discern a fine line around it and assumed this was the edge of the lid. Tools were brought out. The boys chiselled into the fine line and confirmed that indeed they were working on the cover.

There was complete silence among the onlookers as they waited to see what would be inside. After what seemed like an interminable length of time, Ned announced:

"It's coming off!"

A few minutes later the boys lifted the heavy lid. Many pieces of soft cloth were tucked around the contents. Quickly the girls took these out.

Everyone gasped. Below was a white roof.

"It *is* a child's royal coach!" cried Miss Armitage, hardly daring to believe her eyes.

Very gingerly the precious object was lifted from the box. It was fairly heavy.

"This is exquisite!" Aunt Eloise exclaimed. "Look at all those darling little cherubs painted in gold and white."

The shafts for a pony were separately wrapped. They had been cut in half to accommodate them to the small space and laid diagonally across the bottom of the box. Bess ran for mending tape. The shafts were put together and set into place.

Miss Armitage was walking around excitedly. "Can't you just see a darling little girl riding along in this!"

As she finished speaking, there was a hail from the

water and everyone looked up to see Yo arriving in his boat.

"Hello!" Nancy cried excitedly. "Come up here and see what we found!"

If it were possible for anyone's eyes to pop out of his head, this would have happened to Yo when he joined the group. The young man stared, speechless. "You—you pulled the coach up out of the water?"

Nancy smiled. "This is the secret of Mirror Bay!"

"I can't believe it!" he said. "What are you going to do with this—this beautiful thing?"

Miss Armitage told him she planned to present it to the Fenimore Museum. "Of course I'll have to notify the police about this treasure which belonged to an ancestor of mine.

"Yo," she said, "would you go to the museum right now? See if you can find a couple of the officials and bring them here. There's no phone in the cabin, so I can't call."

Yo said he would be delighted to do the errand. When he left, Nancy was deep in thought. Though thrilled by her eventful visit with Aunt Eloise, she was eager to tackle another mystery. The young detective got her wish when called upon to solve *The Double Jinx Mystery*.

An hour later two men arrived from the Fenimore Museum. Mr Clark and Mr Hill were astounded not only at such an unusual gift to the museum, but at Nancy's astuteness and perseverance in solving the mystery. After Miss Armitage had told the history of the child's royal coach, she formally presented it to the museum in care of the two men.

Mr Clark said, "I am not a trustee of the museum,

but I live in Cooperstown and this coach will be a wonderful addition to our exhibits. My congratulations to you, Nancy Drew, and your friends." He smiled. "I'll have a special key made for you. It will be the Key to Cooperstown!"

Nancy thanked him. Then, her eyes twinkling, she added, "And may I please have one to Mirror Bay also?"

The Hardy Boys Mystery Stories

by Franklin W. Dixon

Have you read all the titles in this exciting mystery series? Look out for these new titles coming in 1988:

No. 43 The Bombay Boomerang
No. 44 The Masked Monkey
No. 45 The Shattered Helmet
No. 46 The Clue of the Hissing Serpent

Armada

Good Wives
Louisa M. Alcott

As the four March sisters grow up, their lives lead them in very different directions.

Amy travels the Continent, and Meg settles down to a marriage that is not quite the continual paradise she imagined. Beth, with the secret she tries so hard to hide, stays at home while Jo makes a bold bid for fame and fortune in New York, an adventure which changes the whole course of her life . . .

GOOD WIVES continues the story of the heart-warming March family, begun in LITTLE WOMEN.

Armada

What Katy Did
Susan M. Coolidge

Katy Carr was a tomboy. She hated sewing and darning, her hair was forever in a tangle and her clothes would go and 'tear themselves'.

But secretly Katy longed to be beautiful and patient, to be as kind and gentle as her beloved Cousin Helen.

The story of the dreadful accident that gave Katy the chance to achieve her aim, and how it affected her family – Clover, Elsie, Dorry, Phil, Johnny and Papa – is an enchanting classic which has delighted millions of readers.

Also in Armada

What Katy Did at School
What Katy Did Next

Armada

'JINNY' BOOKS
by Patricia Leitch

When Jinny Manders rescues Shantih, a chestnut Arab, from a
cruel circus, her dreams of owning a horse of her own seem to
come true. But Shantih is wild and unrideable.

This is an exciting and moving series of books about a very
special relationship between a girl and a magnificent horse.

FOR LOVE OF A HORSE
A DEVIL TO RIDE
THE SUMMER RIDERS
NIGHT OF THE RED HORSE
GALLOP TO THE HILLS
HORSE IN A MILLION
THE MAGIC PONY
RIDE LIKE THE WIND
CHESTNUT GOLD
JUMP FOR THE MOON
HORSE OF FIRE

Armada

The Chalet School Series
by Elinor M. Brent-Dyer

Elinor M. Brent-Dyer has written many books about life at the famous Alpine school. Follow the thrilling adventures of Joey, Mary-Lou and all the other well-loved characters in this delightful school series.

Below is a list of Chalet School titles available in Armada. Have you read them all?

The School at the Chalet
Jo of the Chalet School
The Princess of the Chalet School
The Head Girl of the Chalet School
Rivals of the Chalet School
Eustacia Goes to the Chalet School
The Chalet School and Jo
The Chalet Girls in Camp
Exploits of the Chalet Girls
The Chalet School and the Lintons
A Rebel at the Chalet School
The New House at the Chalet School
Jo Returns to the Chalet School
The New Chalet School
The Chalet School in Exile
Three Go to the Chalet School
The Chalet School and the Island
Peggy of the Chalet School
Carola Storms the Chalet School
The Wrong Chalet School

Shocks for the Chalet School
The Chalet School and Barbara
Tom Tackles the Chalet School
Mary-Lou of the Chalet School
A Genius at the Chalet School
Chalet School Fete
A Problem for the Chalet School
The New Mistress at the Chalet School
Excitements at the Chalet School
The Coming of Age of the Chalet School
The Chalet School and Richenda
Trials for the Chalet School
Theodora and the Chalet School
Ruey Richardson at the Chalet School
A Leader in the Chalet School
The Chalet School Wins the Trick
The Feud in the Chalet School
The Chalet School Triplets

Armada

The Hardy Boys Mystery Stories

by Franklin W. Dixon

Have you read all the titles in this exciting mystery series? Look out for these new titles coming in 1987:

No. 41   **The Mysterious Caravan**
No. 42   **Danger on Vampire Trail**
No. 82   **Revenge of the Desert Phantom**
No. 83   **The Skyfire Puzzle**

Armada

The Messenger
Monica Dickens

What is wrong with the house next door? When Rose's parents buy it, to turn into an annexe for the Wood Briar Hotel, they brighten it with cheerful colours and pretty patterns. But the house has a terrible effect on people, filling them with a sense of tragedy and despair. What is the secret of the deep, dark cupboard with its strange smell of the sea? What horror from the past casts its shadow upon the living?

When Rose becomes thirteen – 'that special age' as the surprising Mr Vingo puts it, 'when your mind and spirit are aroused to a state of tempestuous movement' – she is chosen to be a messenger of the Great Grey Horse.

Noble, beautiful and brave, the horse was long ago the favourite charger of the vile Lord of the Moor, and his heroism in the face of treachery saved a whole village. Now he lives on, with a mission to protect innocent people from evil, misery and violence.

A tune played on Mr Vingo's marmalade-coloured piano summons Rose to the horse, and she is galloped back through time into the heart of the mystery. Can she meet the horse's challenge? Can she find a way to break the spell of tragedy? As the horse's messenger she must not fail . . .

This is the first book about Rose and the Great Grey Horse. There are three further titles available in Armada: *Ballad of Favour, The Haunting of Bellamy 4* and *Cry of a Seagull*.

Josephine Pullein-Thompson

The first two novels in a terrific new pony-club series by
this favourite author.

PONY CLUB CUP
The Woodbury Pony Club is a disaster. Its riders and
ponies are the worst in the district. The neighbouring
Cranford Vale team, with its beautifully turned out, well-
schooled ponies, treats them as a joke. And now the
Woodbury members are told that they're getting a
smashed-up jockey as their new instructor. But they're in
for a surprise. For under David Lumley's expert guidance
the Woodbury members begin to work wonders with their
atrocious ponies.

PONY CLUB CHALLENGE
"We've been given a challenge," instructor David Lumley
announces to the Woodbury Pony Club. "To take on the
Cranford Vale in a tetrathlon — swimming, shooting,
running and cross-country riding. Who wants to start
training?" James, Alice, Harry and the others can't bear
to miss the chance to compete against their snooty
neighbours. But is three weeks long enough to get
themselves and their ponies into shape?

Armada